DUNGEON CRAWLERS ACADEMY

BOOK ONE

INTO THE PORTAL

Story by
J.P. SULLIVAN

Art & Coloring by
ELMER DAMASO

Lettering by
NICKY LIM

Original Concept by
JASON DEANGELIS

Coloring Assist: Ma. Cornelia S. Damaso
Cover & Interior Design: Nicky Lim
Interior Layout: Sandy Grayson
Proofreader: B. Lillian Martin
Prepress Technician: Melanie Ujimori
Print Manager: Rhiannon Rasmussen-Silverstein
Production Manager: Lissa Pattillo
Editor-in-Chief: Julie Davis
Associate Publisher: Adam Arnold
Publisher: Jason DeAngelis

Special thanks to Christina McKenzie.

Seven Seas press and purchase enquiries can be sent to Marketing Manager Lianne Sentar at press@gomanga.com. Information regarding the distribution and purchase of digital editions is available from Digital Manager CK Russell at digital@gomanga.com.

Follow Seven Seas Entertainment online at sevenseasentertainment.com.

ISBN: 978-1-64505-978-3
Printed in China
First Printing: June 2022
10 9 8 7 6 5 4 3 2 1

TABLE OF CONTENTS

Chapter One............Page 7

Chapter Two.........Page 69

Chapter Three.......Page 117

Chapter Four........Page 151

Chapter Five........Page 185

Chapter Six.........Page 233

CHAPTER ONE

IT WAS THE BEGINNING OF THE AGE OF MAGIC.

SUSSMAN
QUARRY
A NEW YORK
HISTORIC SITE
CHATTER
CHATTER
THIS FIELD TRIP SUCKS.
WELL, ALMOST.

DID WE GET A FULL HEAD COUNT?

MUSEUM STAFF ONLY
ACTIVE DIG IN
PROGRESS:
HARD HAT AREA!
ACCESS STRICTLY
PROHIBITED
SWING

HWOOOOSH

UHH...
IT'S KIND OF DARK IN THERE.

WEREN'T YOU SOME KIND OF GOTH FIVE MINUTES AGO?
DIFFERENT KIND OF DARKNESS, T.J.!

COME ON. THIS IS AN ADVENTURE.
AND NOT ONE OF THOSE STUPID MAKE-BELIEVE ONES YOU LIKE WITH THE GOBLINS AND EXTRA-SIDED DICE.
CLICK
I, UH... I THINK I'M GOOD.
I'M GONNA HEAD BACK IN BEFORE THEY NOTICE WE'RE GONE.

STOMP

OH, GREAT.

THE WANNABE HALL MONITOR AND HIS *GIRLFRIEND*.
I'M NOT HIS GIRLFRIEND!
AND JUST BECAUSE A DOOR'S THERE *DOESN'T* MEAN YOU HAVE TO OPEN IT. I DON'T UNDERSTAND YOU, T.J.!
WHEEZE!
WHEEZE!
FIGURED I'D FIND YOU WHEREVER NOBODY WAS SUPPOSED TO BE. COME ON, LET'S GO BACK BEFORE YOU ALL GET **DETENTION** OR SOMETHING.

SEE, IF YOU PAID MORE ATTENTION IN CLASS, YOU'D KNOW THEY'RE VERY **INTERESTING** ROCKS.
THIS MUSEUM'S HOME TO A FASCINATING COLLECTION OF LOCALLY-EXCAVATED GEOLOGICAL--
REMIND ME WHY WE LET HIM HANG OUT WITH US AGAIN?
HE'S THE ONLY GUY I KNOW WHO LIKES ROLE-PLAYING GAMES.
I KNOW IT'S A LITTLE HARD TO BELIEVE, BUT THESE GUYS BECAME THE ***GREATEST HEROES*** *THE WORLD HAS EVER SEEN.*

I SWEAR--
CRUNCH

UH-OH.

AAAAAAHH!!
CRRRUMMBLE

WHOMP

ARE YOU GUYS OKAY?

LOOKS LIKE SOME KIND OF RUINS OR SOMETHING.

GO GET HELP!

I DON'T SEE--
INCOMING!
--A WAY OUT.
AWESOME!
THIS GETS BETTER AND BETTER.
......

YEAH. **WAY** COOLER THAN SNEAKING INTO ABANDONED BUILDINGS. THIS IS LIKE *INDIANA JONES* OR SOMETHING.

MAYBE THERE'S TREASURE! WHAT IF WE GOT TO IT FIRST? WE'D BE **RICH**.

WE SHOULD STAY BY THE ENTRANCE. THAT'S THE FIRST PLACE THEY'LL COME LOOKING.

WHO KNOWS HOW FAR DOWN THIS GOES!

WHAT, SCARED OF ANOTHER DROP, DOOFUS?

AND THAT'S JUST FOR STARTERS! HAVE YOU NOTICED HOW *WEIRD* IT IS DOWN HERE?

WHAT DO YOU MEAN?

YEAH, OKAY, MAYBE. BUT NOTHING VENTURED, NOTHING GAINED.

WHOA!

T.J.! WE REALLY, REALLY NEED TO GET OUT OF HERE. RIGHT NOW.
COME ON, IT'S FINE.
NO! YOU DON'T UNDERSTAND. I HAD A...

MAYBE LET'S NOT SAY **"PREMONITION OF DOOM"** OUT LOUD.

I HAVE, LIKE, A REALLY, *REALLY* BAD FEELING ABOUT IT, OKAY?
WE'LL BE FINE.
KNOCK KNOCK
IT'S LOCKED.

NO WORRIES.

I HAPPEN TO BE AN EXPERT ON THIS SUBJECT.
AND THIS GUY HERE'S THE COOLEST OF THEM ALL. T.J. VANCE, THE MASTER THIEF. THEY SAY THERE'S NOWHERE HE CAN'T SNEAK INTO.

AND...
DONE.
CLICK

KIND OF RUSTY, THOUGH. GIVE ME A HAND WITH THIS?
CREAAAK

SHAA

WE'RE DOOMED.
VWEEM

GLARE
AAAAAAHH!!

CHECK IT OUT.

I THINK IT'S CHECKING *US* OUT.
ENTER...

SHOOOM

IF THOU ART WORTHY.

GLEAM

CRAASH

HEY, T.J.! WAIT UP!

EEEEK!

RUN! RUN!

AAAAH!
IT'S GOLD!

ARE YOU SEEING THIS?

DUDE, WE ARE SOOO RICH!

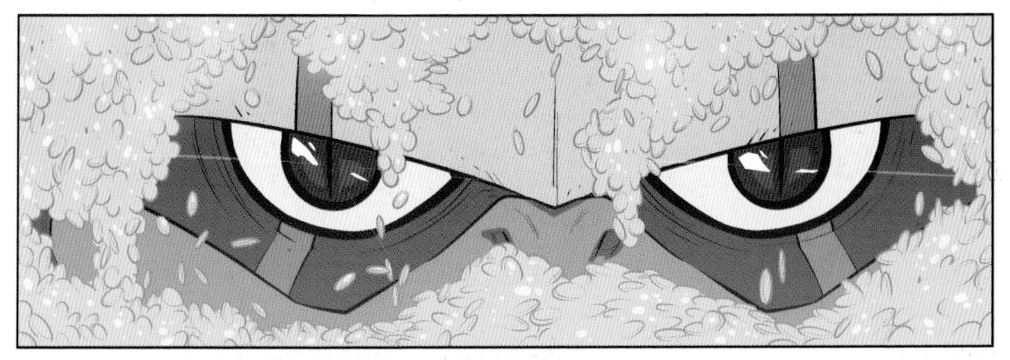

CLINK
CLINK
CLINK
CLINK
CLINK

SO, YEAH. THAT WAS PROBABLY WHEN THE MAGIC REALLY STARTED.

IT'S BEEN...WHAT... **THIRTY YEARS** SINCE THEN?

AWESOME!
THEY'RE SO COOL!

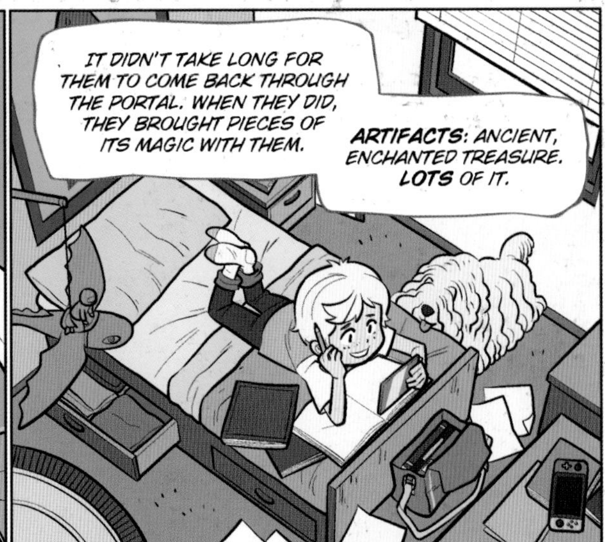
IT DIDN'T TAKE LONG FOR THEM TO COME BACK THROUGH THE PORTAL. WHEN THEY DID, THEY BROUGHT PIECES OF ITS MAGIC WITH THEM.
ARTIFACTS: ANCIENT, ENCHANTED TREASURE. LOTS OF IT.

AT FIRST THEY SHOWED IT OFF...
WOOOOOOOOOO

AND THEN THEY SOLD IT OFF.
AUCTION
ALL SALES
FINAL!
SOTHERBYS
THESE DAYS, ALL YOU NEED TO GET YOUR HANDS ON A GENUINE MAGIC ARTIFACT IS A BIG ENOUGH CHECK.

THEY TRIED TO SEND ALL KINDS OF EXPERTS IN THERE TO GET THEIR HANDS ON THEM. THE WORLD'S TOUGHEST TOUGH GUYS.
BUT THERE WAS ONE SMALL PROBLEM.

YOU ARE... UNWORTHY.

UNWORTHY.

UN! WORTHY!
CLOUT

NO MATTER WHO THEY SENT--AND THEY SENT THOUSANDS--THE PORTAL WOULD ONLY ACCEPT **ONE** KIND OF PERSON.
YOU MAY ENTER.

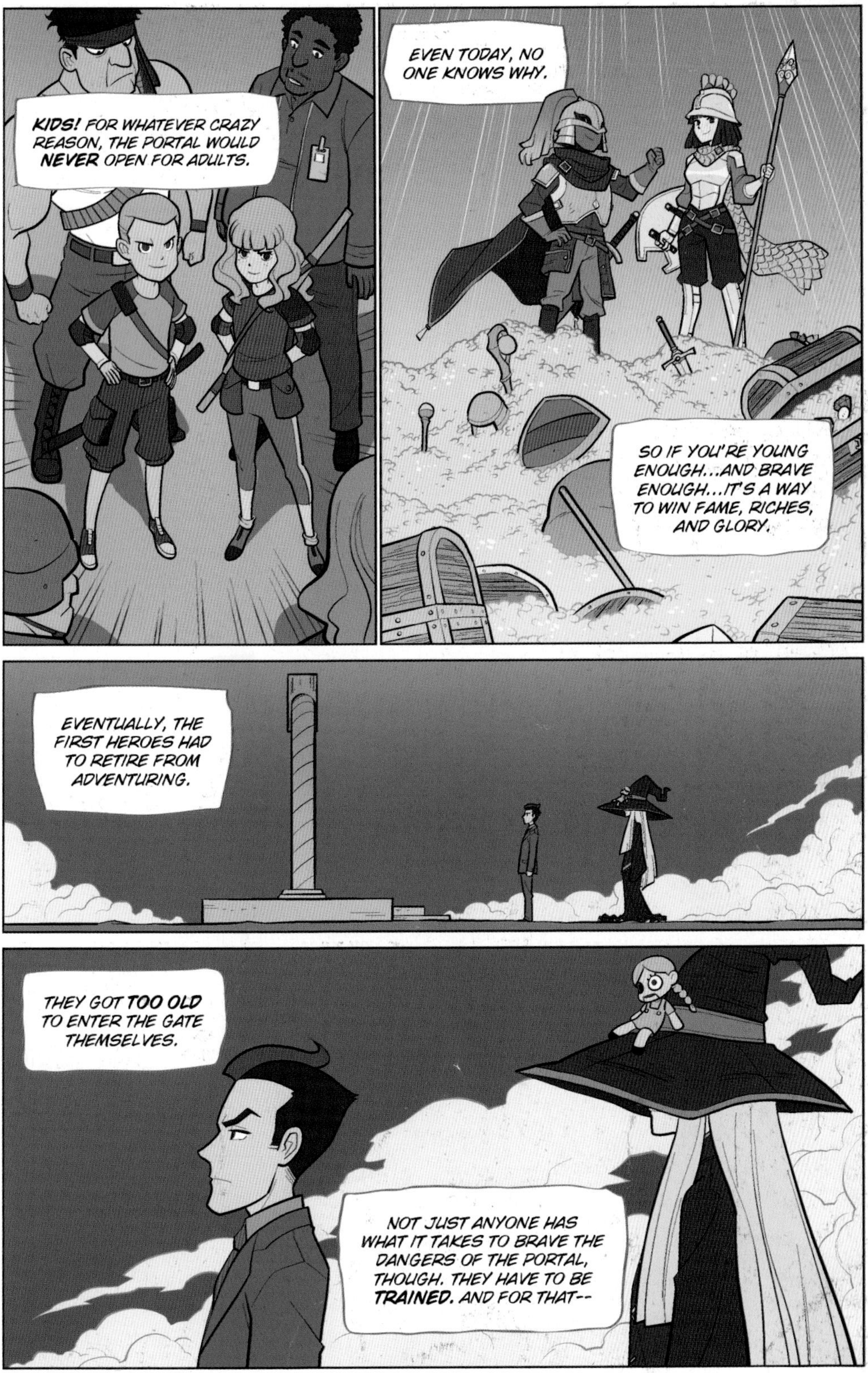

KIDS! FOR WHATEVER CRAZY REASON, THE PORTAL WOULD **NEVER** OPEN FOR ADULTS.

EVEN TODAY, NO ONE KNOWS WHY.

SO IF YOU'RE YOUNG ENOUGH...AND BRAVE ENOUGH...IT'S A WAY TO WIN FAME, RICHES, AND GLORY.

THEY MADE A SCHOOL.

DUNGEON CRAWLERS ACADEMY

Prepare for Adventure!

DING-A-LING
I WANT TO BE AN ADVENTURER.
YEAH, YOU AND EVERYONE ELSE, KID.
WHAT'RE YOUR QUALIFICATIONS? YOU KNOW HOW TO FIGHT? QUICK ON YOUR FEET? GOOD WITH MAGIC TRICKS?
WELL, UH...
ENLIST NOW!

GOT ANYONE TO VOUCH FOR YOU?
MY ART TEACHER WROTE A NICE LETTER OF REFERENCE...?
SIGH!
TAP TAP

NEXT YOU'RE GOING TO ASK FOR THE MAGIC TEST, RIGHT? EVERYONE DOES. HOLD OUT YOUR HAND, KID.
IS THIS THING MAGIC?
OOOH!
YEAH, YEAH, ALAKAZAM, WHATEVER.
LET'S GET THIS OVER WITH.

BUT WHAT DOES IT *DO*?
IT MEASURES YOUR **TALENT** FOR HOCUS-POCUS.
MOST PEOPLE DON'T EVEN HAVE A *SINGLE SPARK* OF MAGIC IN THEM.

POOMF
!

OH! LOOK!
WELL. LOOKS LIKE YOU HAVE, IN FACT, EXACTLY--

ONE.

SINGLE.

SPARK OF MAGIC.
THEN...!

DUNGEON CRAWLER'S ACADEMY
APPLICANT:
NATHAN GREENE
F-
PROCTOR'S ASSESSMENT:
NOT SUITABLE FOR TRAINING
IT'S OKAY, HONEY. LOOK, I KNOW IT'S HARD, BUT BEING A HERO IS A REALLY, *REALLY* DANGEROUS JOB! PEOPLE **DIE** DOING IT SOMETIMES, YOU KNOW.

THERE'S LOTS OF OTHER OPTIONS. ARE YOU STILL THINKING ABOUT ART SCHOOL?
SIGH...

YEAH... I GUESS.
BESIDES! ADVENTURING. DUNGEON-DIVING. THERE'S NO FUTURE IN IT! YOU'D BE LIKE A WASHED-UP LINEBACKER, ONLY *WORSE.*
WHAT'RE YOU SUPPOSED TO DO WHEN YOUR QUESTING YEARS ARE OVER?

T.J. VANCE IS PROBABLY LIKE THE *RICHEST GUY* IN THE WORLD, DAD.
I BET HE DOES PRETTY MUCH WHATEVER HE WANTS!
NOT EVERYBODY'S MEANT TO BE A HERO, NATHAN. YOU GOT INTO A VERY NICE HIGH SCHOOL. HOW'S THAT WORKING OUT FOR YOU?

HYUCK!
HYUCK!
HEE HEE!

HA HA!
EEEEEEW!
HA HA HA HA!
HA
AUGH?!
OH NO
PLOOF

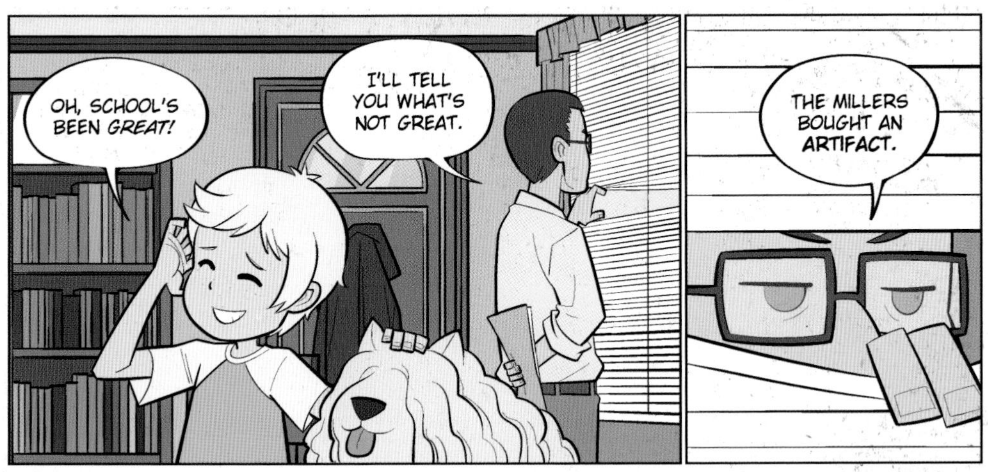
OH, SCHOOL'S BEEN *GREAT!*
I'LL TELL YOU WHAT'S NOT GREAT.
THE MILLERS BOUGHT AN **ARTIFACT.**

PSHEW
HA HA! LAWNMOWERS ARE FOR SUCKERS!

HOW THE HECK DID THEY AFFORD IT?
SNAP
THEY PROBABLY MAXED OUT THEIR CREDIT CARDS.
DO YOU KNOW HOW EXPENSIVE THOSE THINGS ARE? EVEN THE CHEAPEST MAGIC DOOHICKEYS ARE **MONTHS** OF MY SALARY!
WRING

THEY'RE HOLDING ANOTHER AUCTION RIGHT HERE ON LONG ISLAND. LIKE WE NEED MORE **MANIACS** RUNNING AROUND WITH *FLAMING SWORDS.*
THEY ARE?!
THWAP

T.J. VANCE, HERO AND LEGENDARY ADVENTURER, will soon open the doors to a stunning bazaar of the fantastic. The very finest Artifacts—procured by the mightiest heroes—can all be yours at reasonable installment rates. Don't let your dreams die! Write your own legendary destiny!
OPEN TO THE PUBLIC!
Behold with your own eyes the majesty of a genuine, fire-breathing dragon!

NO THANKS. I'LL STAY HOME AND WATCH THE GAME AND PRETEND THE WORLD STILL MAKES SENSE.
YOU KNOW, DEAR, MAGIC'S NOT *ALL* BAD. GLADYS WAS TELLING ME...
MASSAGE
MASSAGE

MAYBE YOU ALWAYS DREAMED OF BEING ABLE TO FLY? THESE **WINGED SHOES** WILL SEND YOU SOARING TO NEW HEIGHTS AS SOON AS YOU TIE THE LACES!

HIKE THE ROCKIES WITH THE THERMOS OF ENDLESS WATER AND THE CUP OF NEVER SPILLING!
THIS COAT OF MANY CLIMATES, PERFECT FOR WINTER SNOW AND SUMMER SUN!
OH NO
OR THIS TRULY RARE ARTIFACT: A PILLOW OF PERPETUAL FLUFFINESS!
OOH! AAH!

CHUCK, THIS IS *INCREDIBLE!* I CAN STILL BARELY BELIEVE IT'S FOR REAL.
DID YOU KNOW IT WAS ONLY FIVE YEARS AGO THAT THEY STARTED LETTING REGULAR PEOPLE BUY THEIR OWN ARTIFACTS?
"REGULAR PEOPLE"...? IT'S GREAT IF YOU HAVE LIKE A MILLION BILLION DOLLARS.
WE CAN'T AFFORD THIS STUFF, NATHAN.
OH NO
THE LANTERN OF ILLUSTRIOUS LUMINANCE
Opening Bid: $10,000
THIS IS, LIKE, THE CHEAPEST THING HERE. SEE THE PRICE TAG?

THE LANTERN OF ILLUSTRIOUS LUMINANCE! OPENING BID: $10,000!
OH NO
AND IT'S ONLY A MAGIC LANTERN. LITERALLY ALL IT DOES IS *GLOW*.
AWESOME!

THIS GENUINE **WIZARD'S STAFF.**

FLASH

FLASH

IF YOU HAD THIS? YOU COULD CHANNEL ALL THE POWER OF THE ARCANE. YOU'D BE A GENUINE **MAGICIAN.**

FLASH

AN ARTIFACT THIS POWERFUL HAS NEVER BEEN SOLD TO THE GENERAL PUBLIC BEFORE!

ENZO HERE HAS SUCCESSFULLY COMPLETED OVER A HUNDRED QUESTS BEYOND THE GATE.

AND HIS MOST DARING ADVENTURE YET?

P'TUI!

AWWW!

IT WAS A LOT BIGGER WHEN I FOUGHT IT.
GRUMBLE

MAN, THAT DOESN'T LOOK **ANYTHING** LIKE THE AD!
IT'S ADORABLE!

ONE MILLION!
TWO MILLION!
THREE MILLION FROM THE SAN DIEGO ZOO!

YOU SHOULD DRAW IT. WHEN ARE YOU GOING TO GET ANOTHER CHANCE TO DRAW A REAL DRAGON?
WAY AHEAD OF YOU!
SCRITCH SCRATCH

BLINK

DOOOOM

YEAH, WE DRAGGED IT THROUGH THE GATE, AND, AFTER THAT, IT JUST KIND OF STARTED **SHRINKING**.
MAYBE EARTH JUST ISN'T MAGICAL ENOUGH FOR DRAGONS? WHO KNOWS.
OH NO
GULP!
NATHAN... YOU OKAY?

O-OH MY GOD! IT'S HORRIBLE! DID YOU SEE IT?! DID YOU SEE IT?!

? ?
OH NO

BLINK
BLINK

YOU ARE SUCH A WIMP, NATHAN.
Y-Y-YOU DON'T UNDERSTAND! WE'VE GOTTA GET AWAY FROM IT! RIGHT NOW!
OH, FOR PETE'S SAKE. IT'S JUST AN OVERGROWN LIZARD. THE WHOLE THING'S A SCAM.
EXCUSE ME?!
OH NO

SEE, WATCH. I BET IT DOESN'T EVEN BITE.
DON'T EVEN *THINK* ABOUT IT!
OH HO

HEY! WAKE UP!

FOOOOM

EEEE!

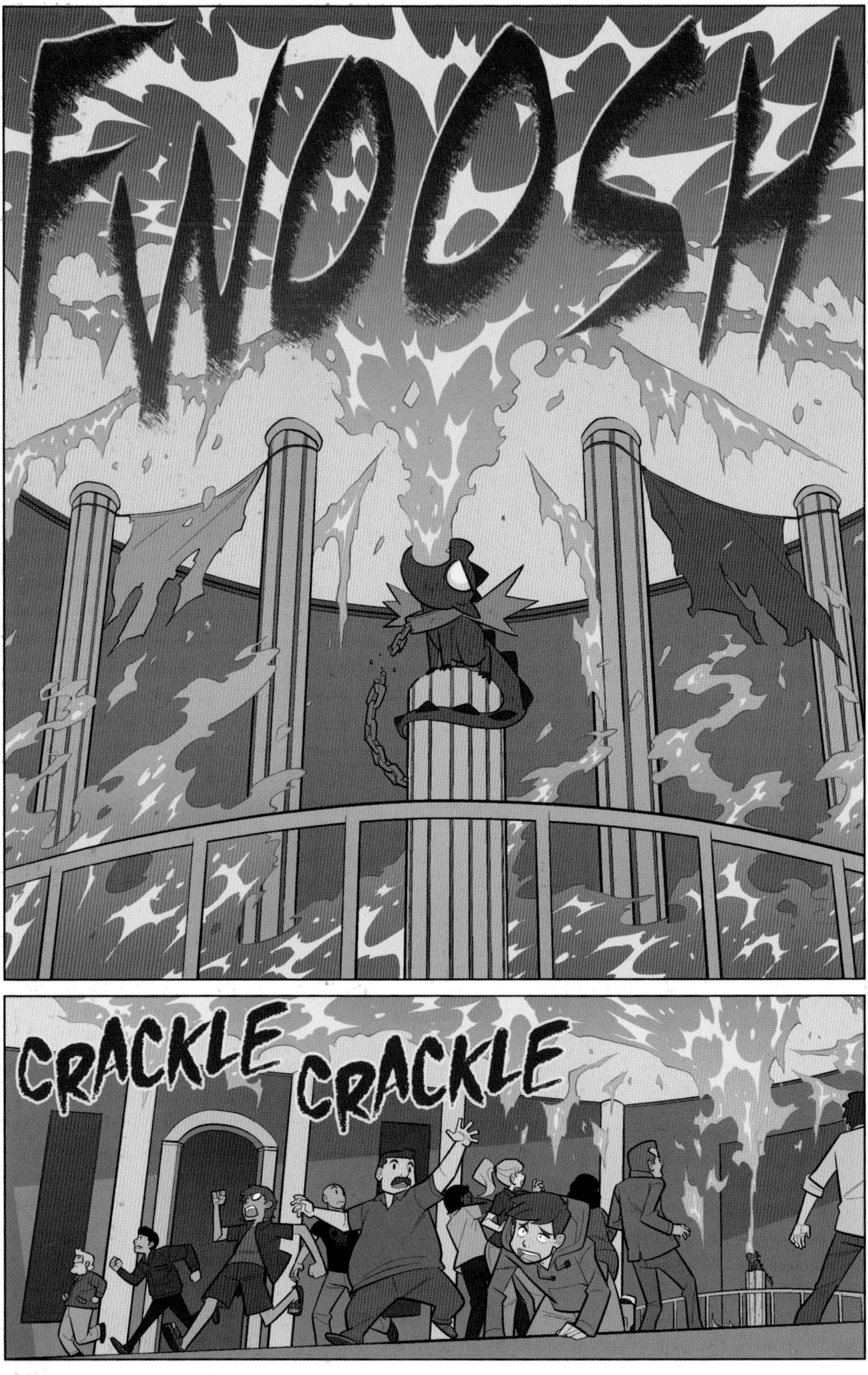

FWOOSH

CHUCK! ARE YOU OKAY?!
MOVE IT!

COME ON!
LEER
THUMP

SHOW ME WHAT YOU'VE--

!
FLOP

WHAM

CRACKLE
CRACKLE
CHUCK!

OH NO

RRR...

GRRR!

WE NEED **HELP** OVER HERE!

EVERYONE, STAY CALM!
GET IN THERE, ENZO! WE'RE ***NOT*** LOSING THAT LIZARD!

SO, MY BEST FRIEND WAS ABOUT TO BE EATEN ALIVE. NOT MY BEST TUESDAY.

BUMP

I GUESS THERE WAS MAYBE SOMETHING ELSE I COULD HAVE DONE.

AND I SAID **YES.**

GRRRR?
HIIISSSS!
FOOO

FWSHH

GULP!
AAAAAA

AAAAAAA...!

HEH!
?!

PANT!
PANT!

BAD DOG.

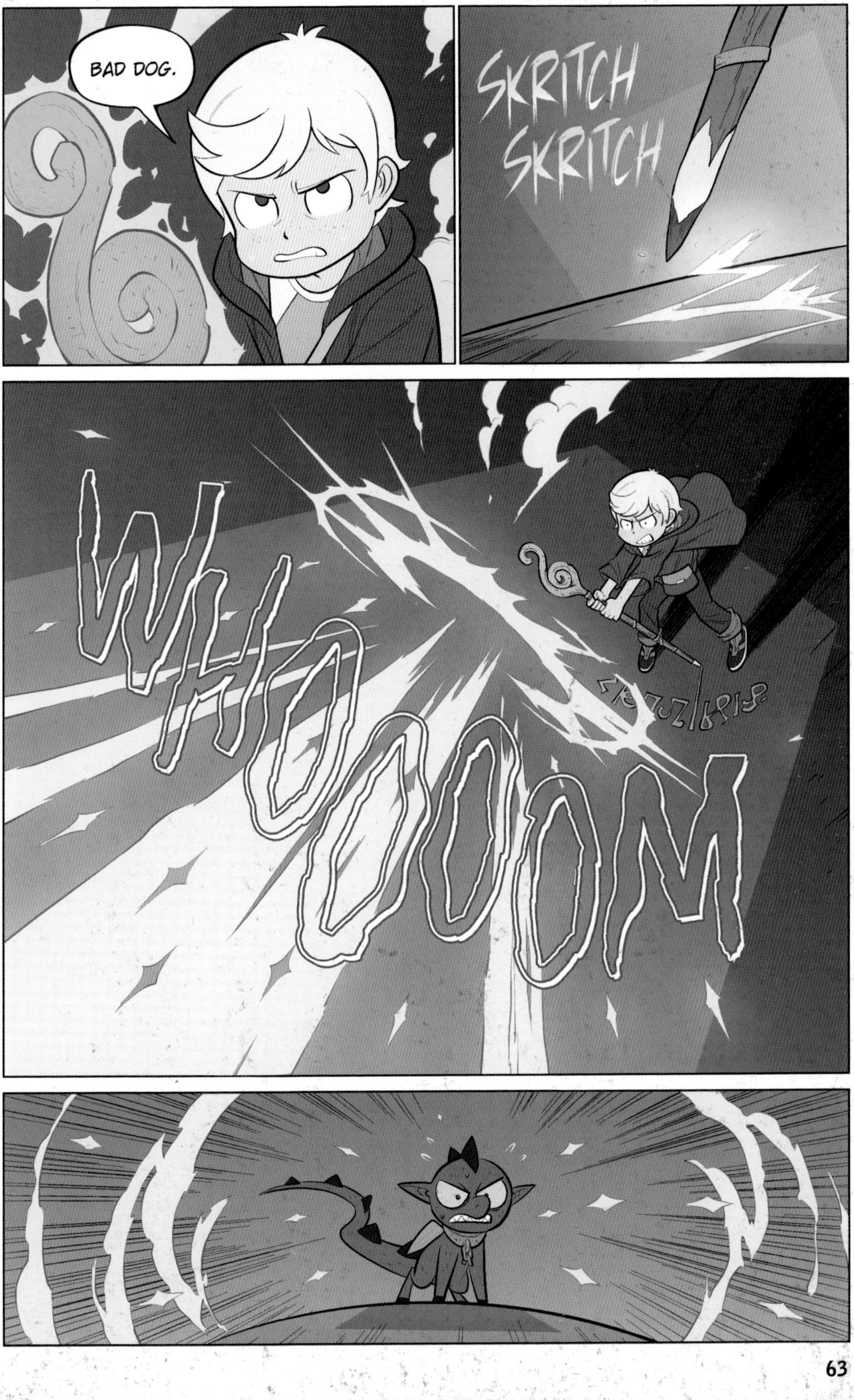

SKRITCH
SKRITCH

WHOOOOM

TINK

PLONK

WOBBLE
WOBBLE

WHUMP

WOW, KID! YOU'RE A **NATURAL!**
D-DID I... DID I REALLY JUST DO THAT?

DALEY CONVENTION CENTER
RESCUE

OH

DON'T WORRY. ALL OF THESE BURNS SHOULD HEAL.
BUT MY **BOXERS** ARE SHOWING...!

CONGRATS, KID. YOU'RE THE HERO OF THE DAY.
MR. VANCE! WELL, I, *ER*...I JUST DID WHAT I, YOU KNOW, THINK THAT ANYBODY WOULD'VE DONE IN MY POSITION, AND--

NICE **STAFF**, ISN'T IT?
TOP OF THE LINE PIECE OF EQUIPMENT.

OH! HERE YOU GO.

YEAH, DOESN'T WORK LIKE THAT. ANYONE EVER TELL YOU HOW THIS STUFF WORKS?
YOU USED THE ARTIFACT, SO IT'S ATTUNED TO YOU NOW.
WAIT, WHAT...? WHAT DOES THAT MEAN?

THAT YOU'RE A HERO, OF COURSE. A MAGE. A HOLDER OF ANCIENT MAGIC. FEELS GREAT, DON'T IT?
I, UH--
NOW THAT IT'S ATTUNED TO YOU, IT MEANS THAT NO ONE ELSE WILL EVER BE ABLE TO USE THAT STAFF.
IT ALSO MEANS YOU OWE ME...

FIVE MILLION DOLLARS.

HERE'S THE HERO OF THE DAY, PEOPLE!
FLASH
FLASH

COME ON, KID. SMILE FOR THE CAMERAS.
DON'T WORRY. I THINK THIS'LL WORK OUT NICELY FOR BOTH OF US.

YOU ALWAYS WANTED TO BE AN **ADVENTURER,** RIGHT?
WELL, CAREFUL WHAT YOU WISH FOR...

CHAPTER TWO

The Dungeon Crawlers Academy.

ZACH, I AM DEEPLY **DISAPPOINTED** IN YOU.

YOU GIVING ME DETENTION OR SOMETHING? YOU DON'T EVEN HAVE A GOOD REASON.

RIGHT. *REASONS.* LET'S TALK ABOUT THE REASONS, SHALL WE?

YOU WERE LATE TO CLASS AT LEAST A DOZEN TIMES.
ZZZ!
GOT INTO FIGHTS WITH FELLOW STUDENTS ON *FIVE* SEPARATE OCCASIONS.
FLAGRANTLY IGNORED ALL ESTABLISHED RULES AND SAFETY PROCEDURES.
ILLEGALLY ENTERED THE PORTAL WITHOUT PROPER FACULTY SUPERVISION.

AND TO MAKE MATTERS WORSE!
YOU PUNCHED A **TEACHER** IN THE FACE.
IT WAS AN ACCIDENT. WE WERE **SPARRING.**

ONE MORE SCREW-UP! AND YOU ARE **GONE**. FOREVER! DO YOU UNDERSTAND ME?

I DON'T CARE HOW HIGH YOU SCORE IN COMBAT TESTS. YOU ARE ON **PROBATION,** AND THAT ONLY ENDS WHEN I SAY IT DOES.

FINE. WE DONE HERE? I'VE GOT HOMEWORK TO DO. SINCE I'M A MODEL STUDENT, STARTING RIGHT NOW.

THERE IS ONE OTHER THING.

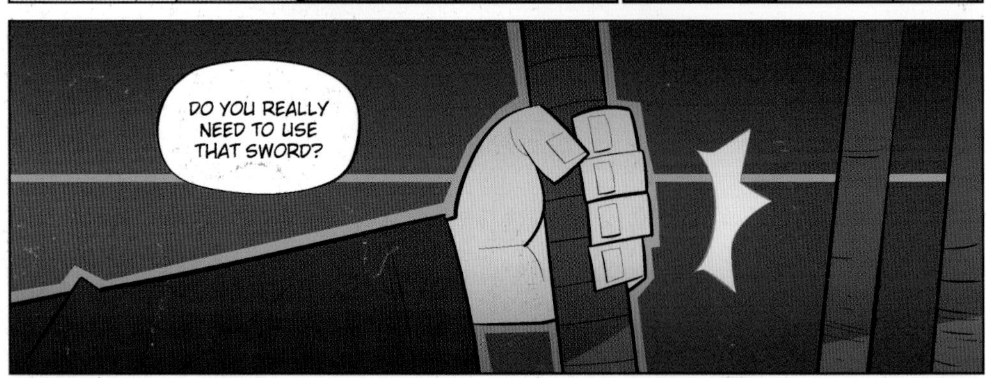

MANDY, YOU CONSISTENTLY EARN **TOP MARKS** IN ALL ACADEMIC SUBJECTS, AND YOU'VE WON PRAISE FROM ALL YOUR TEACHERS.

WE'RE EXPECTING **BIG THINGS** FROM YOU IN THE YEAR'S FIRST PORTAL EXPEDITION.

WELL, *GOSH*, SIR. I WOULDN'T CALL MYSELF THE BEST, BUT IT SURE IS **NICE** TO HEAR YOU SAY SO!

WE BELIEVE YOU'VE ALREADY GOT WHAT IT TAKES TO GO ON YOUR FIRST ADVENTURE.

WOW! YOU'RE SO KIND.

EVERY GROUP NEEDS AN EXPERT IN LOCKS AND TRAPS...AND WHILE I HATE PUTTING IT LIKE THIS, IT'S CLEAR YOU'VE GOT A **KNACK** FOR THIEVERY.
"THIEF" IS SUCH A HARSH WORD, PRINCIPAL WALKER, SIR. I THINK OF MYSELF AS... AN "ADVENTUROUS ARCHAEOLOGIST!"

CERTAINLY HAS A NICER RING TO IT.
I THINK WE'RE DONE HERE.
UNLESS THERE'S ANYTHING *ELSE* YOU'D LIKE TO MENTION?
NOPE!

SIGH...

YUP!
I REALLY AM THE BEST!
HA
HA
HA!

DOING A LITTLE "ARCHAEOLOGY" IN MY TROPHY CASE, WERE YOU?
I STOLE THIS STUFF FAIR AND SQUARE!
MINE!
MINE!

YOU ARE TWO HUNDRED PERCENT ON PROBATION.
ALSO, YOU'RE GROUNDED.
YOU'RE NOT MY REAL DAD!!
STOMP
STOMP

I SWEAR. HOLDING BACK MONSTERS FIVE TIMES MY SIZE WAS EASIER THAN RUNNING A SCHOOL.
VRRN
VRRN RRN

WHAT'S THAT? A TRANSFER STUDENT?

SO YOU'RE A WIZARD NOW?
UH...NOT EXACTLY, BUT KIND OF?
AND YOU SLAYED A DRAGON.
KIND OF.

OUR BOY WAS ON TV! DID YOU SEE HIM?!
AND THEY LET YOU HAVE THAT THING FOR FREE?
KIND OF?
WOOF! WOOF!
AND NOW YOU WANT TO GO OUT AND RISK YOUR LIFE ON THE OTHER SIDE OF A PORTAL THAT GOES TO A **DIFFERENT WORLD.**

THAT ABOUT SUMS IT UP, YEAH.
SON, I HOPE YOU WON'T TAKE THIS THE WRONG WAY, BUT YOU DO *NOT* STRIKE ME AS THE ADVENTUROUS TYPE.
WOW! HE ZAPPED THAT THING REAL GOOD!
WOOF! WOOF

PAT PAT

YOU KNOW, I ALWAYS DID TELL YOUR MOTHER THAT THERE WAS SOMETHING TO ALL OF THIS MAGIC STUFF.

WOOF! WOOF!

WOW!
IT'S EVEN BIGGER THAN I THOUGHT.
THERE'S A LOT THAT GOES ON HERE. TRAINING, RESEARCH...

AND **ADVENTURE**, OF COURSE.
I KNOW EVERYTHING ABOUT IT!
I WATCHED ALL THOSE WEBFLIX DOCUMENTARIES YOU DID.

THOSE WERE T.J.'S IDEA.
I'M NOT SURE HE ALWAYS GIVES THE RIGHT IMPRESSION.
HE, *UH*, SEEMS TO CARE A LOT ABOUT **MONEY**.
THAT'S EXACTLY WHAT I MEAN. VANCE AND HIS RAIDERS MIGHT BE OBSESSED WITH LOOT, BUT I HAVE *OTHER* PRIORITIES. AND SO DO OUR BEST STUDENTS.
SQUEAK SQUEAK

THIS ACADEMY WAS FOUNDED TO DISCOVER ***WHY*** THE DUNGEON EXISTS.
A LABYRINTH FULL OF ARTIFACTS AND MAGICAL BEASTS, AS BIG AS A WHOLE WORLD? IT'S BEEN TWENTY YEARS AND WE'RE *STILL* JUST SCRATCHING THE SURFACE!
YEAH! I ALWAYS WONDERED. WHERE DID THE PEOPLE WHO BUILT IT **GO?** WHY DID THEY BUILD IT IN THE FIRST PLACE?
WHY ARE ONLY KIDS ALLOWED IN? IT DOESN'T MAKE ANY SENSE!

YOU'RE ASKING ALL THE RIGHT QUESTIONS. I WONDER THE SAME MYSELF.
PEOPLE LIKE US, WE'RE HERE TO DISCOVER THE **TRUTH,** NOT STRIKE IT RICH.

$5,000,000
I DON'T THINK ME BEING RICH IS *EVER* GOING TO BE A PROBLEM.

WELCOME TO THE
DUNGEON CRAWLERS ACADEMY

IT GETS A LITTLE HECTIC SOMETIMES, AND IT'S NOT FLUSH WITH GOVERNMENT MONEY LIKE NATALIA'S INSTITUTE OUT IN TEXAS, BUT I THINK OUR SCHOOL HAS ITS OWN *UNIQUE* CHARM.

AAAH!
OOOH!
HMPH!
GRRR!

WE'VE GOT A SMALL PROBLEM.
DON'T WE ALWAYS?
YOU REMEMBER HOW WE WRANGLED THOSE **BASILISKS** FOR CLASS? THE SPIKY ONES WITH ALL THE POKEY BITS?
YES, PROFESSOR WILLIS.

ONE OF THEM *MAAAY* HAVE GOTTEN LOOSE IN THE FOURTH-YEAR DORMS.
SIGH...
WE REALLY NEED TO DO SOMETHING ABOUT THESE SENIOR PRANKS.
CRICK
CRACK

GRUNT!

WHOOSH

OH, COME ON! THE REST OF US STILL HAVE TO *WALK!*
UHHH...

WHERE AM I SUPPOSED TO TAKE THIS?
JINGLE JINGLE

POOF

HI THERE!
YOU'RE NATHAN! THE NEW MAGIC USER, RIGHT? A COUPLE OF US SAW YOU ON TV.
WHOA!
JINGLE JINGLE

OOH, IS THAT THE STAFF? CAN I SEE?

OH, SURE!
ZIIIP

IT'S SO MAGICAL!
IT SURE IS... BUT I DON'T REALLY KNOW HOW TO USE IT.

WELL, THAT'S WHY YOU'RE **HERE,** DUMMY! SO YOU CAN LEARN.
THOUGH, HONESTLY, YOU COULD HAVE FOOLED ME!
HA HA HA!
HA HA HA!
JINGLE JINGLE

HERE, TAKE THIS AND THIS AND THIS AND THIS...
POOF POOF POOF POOF
AH!

CAN'T FORGET THIS ONE, EITHER! ***THE OMNIBUS ARCANE.*** EVERY ASPIRING MAGE NEEDS ONE!
MAKE SURE YOU ALWAYS BRING IT TO CLASS, OKAY?
THE OMNIBUS ARCANE
BEING A COMPLETE GUIDE TO SPELLS, ENCHANTMENTS, MAGIC, WIZARDRY, AND THAUMATURGICAL PRESTIDIGITATION
BY MAXIMILIAN DONENSTONE

YOU KNOW, YOU'RE KIND OF **SHORT** FOR FOURTEEN.
DID YOU LIE ABOUT YOUR AGE TO GET IN?
UH...CAN WE JUST SAY I'M A LATE BLOOMER?
WHATEVER! THIS WAY.
CLACK

YOU'RE GOING TO HAVE A LOT OF CATCHING UP TO DO, YOU KNOW.
WE HAVE A FEW PEOPLE HERE WHO'VE BEEN TRAINING SINCE THEY WERE TEN.
OH, I'M **ASHA**, BY THE WAY. I'M A MAGE, TOO! THE PRINCIPAL TOLD ME TO SHOW YOU AROUND. YOU CAN SEE THE DORMS UP AHEAD.
I CAN'T EVEN **SEE** WHERE I'M GOING!
HA HA! SURE YOU CAN!

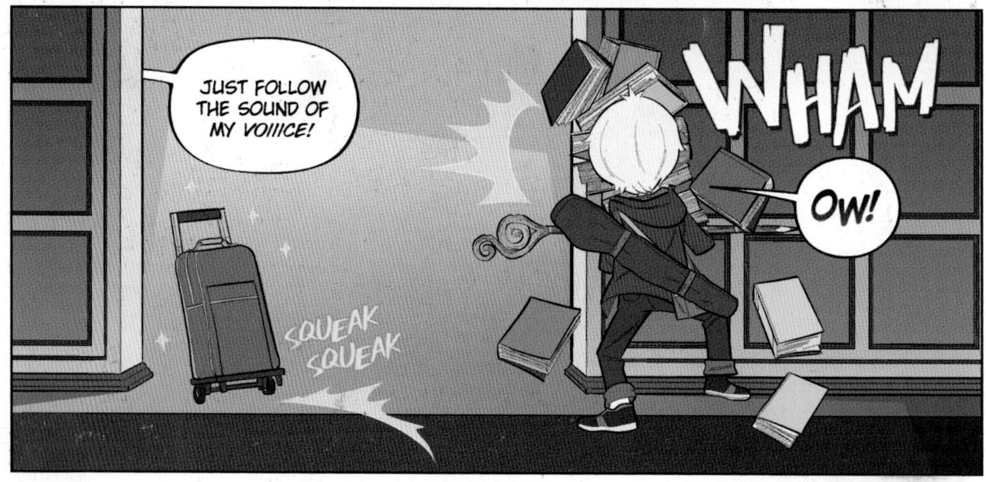
JUST FOLLOW THE SOUND OF MY *VOIIICE!*
WHAM
OW!
SQUEAK SQUEAK

SHIIIK

I'M DYING.
WIZARDS *DO* TEND TO BE IN TERRIBLE SHAPE. I GUESS YOU'RE ALREADY A NATURAL!

I COULD USE A **NAP**. WHEN'S CLASS?
OH...IN FIVE MINUTES?

I'LL BE RIGHT THERE...
WHOMP

WHO'S THIS LOSER?

NICE TO MEET YOU...?

HEY, WATCH IT, BUB!
SORRY, EXCUSE ME. PARDON.
HE'S THE ONE WHO STOPPED THE DRAGON!
YOUR NEW BOYFRIEND?
RUDE.
ZZZ

IS GARETT LATE TO CLASS **AGAIN?**
WHO'S GARETT?

HE'S NOT SITTING HERE, IS HE?
NAH!
HE'S OUR DUNGEONEERING TEACHER. HE'S...

YAAAWN...

...A LITTLE UNIQUE.
YOU'RE LATE.

NICE THING ABOUT BEING A TEACHER IS THAT CLASS NEVER STARTS UNTIL I GET HERE. CAN'T BE LATE IF I DECIDE WHAT LATE IS.

NOW, LET'S SEE HERE...WE HAVE... A TRANSFER STUDENT, IS IT?
FLIP
FLAP
FLAP

NATHAN GREENE, GET UP HERE.
YES, SIR!

SOME OF THEM SURE DO DRESS WEIRD.
DOES THAT GUY REALLY NEED TO WEAR THE HOOD INDOORS?

GO AHEAD AND TELL US SOMETHING ABOUT YOURSELF.
UH. HI. I'M NATHAN. I, UH, DRAW SUFF. AND, UM...DO MAGIC, I GUESS?

RIGHT. NOT MUCH FOR PUBLIC SPEAKING. I'LL MAKE A NOTE OF THAT.

ANYWAY, LET'S SEE...DEFEATED A DRAGON...WIELDS A TOP-GRADE ARTIFACT...
THE FIRST SPELL HE EVER CAST WAS OF THE THIRD CIRCLE...

HOLY MOLY, PEOPLE. THIS GUY IS THE REAL DEAL!
WAIT, WHAT?!

EVERYBODY, STUFF YOUR BOOKS AWAY! WE NEED TO SEE THIS GUY'S MAGIC **FIRST-HAND!**
YOU DON'T GET IT! THE DRAGON THING WAS KIND OF A *SPECIAL CASE.* LIKE--I GOT LUCKY.
I JUST KIND OF WAVED MY STAFF AND SUDDENLY--

WE'RE OFF TO THE MAZE, EVERYONE!
YEAH! AWESOME!
ALL RIGHT!
"THE MAZE?" WHAT'S THE MAZE?

YOU'LL SEE!
IT'S HORRIFYING!
HEH!

WHAT... IS IT?
A MAN-MADE SIMULATED DUNGEON-SPACE DESIGNED TO TEST STUDENT ABILITY UNDER REALISTIC ADVENTURING CONDITIONS.

IT'S THE WORLD'S CRAZIEST OBSTACLE COURSE!
THAT DOESN'T SOUND TOO BAD. IT'S **SAFE,** RIGHT?
EVERYONE ELSE IN CLASS A MANAGED TO BEAT IT.

SOME EVEN MANAGED *WITHOUT* GETTING KILLED!
CAN I JUST POINT OUT THAT THIS IS MY **FIRST DAY?**

I GIVE YOU:
THE MAZE!
CLANK
CLANK

CLICK
CRUNCH
NOBODY REALLY DIES IN THIS THING, RIGHT?
CRACK
GRIND

IT WASN'T SO LONG AGO I WAS A YOUNG ADVENTURER MYSELF...
THERE I WAS, CRAWLING DOWN A SHEER CLIFF FACE IN A DRIPPING CAVERN, WHEN A **GIANT SPIDER** JUMPED ONTO MY BACK!
AAAAAH!

IT CAME AT ME WITH ITS **FANGS,** BUT I GRABBED THEM WITH BOTH HANDS, AND--
AAAAHH!
SHAKE
UH, SIR! I-I'M NOT A SPIDER.
SHAKE
AH.

SORRY, KID. I LOST MYSELF FOR A SECOND THERE.
SO WHAT DO YOU SAY? READY TO GIVE IT A **TRY?**

OKAY, ME. LET'S HAVE A THINK.

A REAL HERO WOULD **NEVER** SHY AWAY FROM A CHALLENGE JUST BECAUSE IT'S HARD.

BUT I'M **NOT** A REAL HERO. WHAT KIND OF CRAZY DUMB REASON WOULD MAKE SOMEBODY THROW HIMSELF IN THERE?

I CAN'T WAIT TO SEE WHAT YOU CAN DO.
LEAN
I WAS BORN READY!

I ALREADY REGRET THIS!
AH HA HA HA!

NOW THAT'S WHAT I LIKE TO HEAR!
KA-CHUNK

WHIR
CLICK
CLICK

POP

VRRRT
VRRRT
VRRRT
BWEEM
CLONK

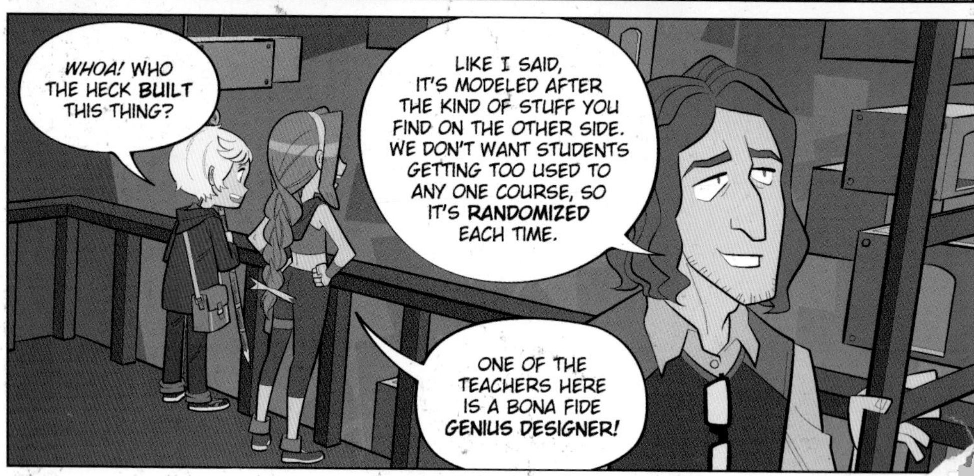
WHOA! WHO THE HECK **BUILT** THIS THING?
LIKE I SAID, IT'S MODELED AFTER THE KIND OF STUFF YOU FIND ON THE OTHER SIDE. WE DON'T WANT STUDENTS GETTING TOO USED TO ANY ONE COURSE, SO IT'S **RANDOMIZED** EACH TIME.
ONE OF THE TEACHERS HERE IS A BONA FIDE **GENIUS DESIGNER!**

ANYWAY, THE PRINCIPAL WON'T LET YOU GO THROUGH THE PORTAL UNTIL YOU PROVE YOU CAN HANDLE AT LEAST *THIS MUCH* TROUBLE, SO GET TO IT!
CREAK CREAK

CREAK
CREAK
CREAK

THUD

YEAH, *THAT* DOESN'T LOOK FOREBODING AT ALL.

DON'T WORRY! IF IT LOOKS LIKE YOU'RE GOING TO DIE OR SOMETHING, I CAN **STOP** THE TEST!

GEE, THANKS.

OH MAN!
OH MAN!

WE DO NEED TO MAKE THIS A LITTLE MORE INTERESTING, THOUGH.
LISTEN UP. I'VE GOT AN IDEA.
HARRUMPH!

DEATH
DESTRUCTION
DON'T EVEN THINK ABOUT IT!

DESTRUCTION

WELL, HERE WE GO.

RUUUMMMBLE
WHOOOOA!

WAAAH!
AH!
CLICK

EEK!
SNAP
SNAP

THUNK
THUNK
THUNK
AAAAGH!

PANT!
PANT!
PHEW! I THINK THIS HAS TO BE THE LAST ROOM, RIGHT?

PANT! PANT!
PANT!
WHEEZE!
ALMOST THERE...
STOMP
DUN
DUUUNNNN
ME.
NOT QUITE. THERE'S STILL THE BOSS.

HEY, YOU'RE EVEN SHORTER THAN ME.
OH, YOU ARE SO DEAD.

UHHH...SO I JUST HAVE TO GET PAST YOU?
TRY ME. I DARE YOU.
HEY, WHAT'S THAT?!

DART
EXIT
HUH?

GLINT

SWING

THWAP

BUMP
BOP
OOF!
EEP!
WAUGH!
WHOMP

FWUMP
OWWW!

YOU DON'T HAVE A CHANCE. WHY DON'T YOU GIVE UP AND GO HOME?

COME ON, DON'T HOLD BACK! USE YOUR **MAGIC!**
HE'S BEEN TRAINED TO WITHSTAND IT!

*YEAH, EXCEPT I HAVEN'T BEEN TRAINED TO **USE** IT.*

NATHAN! DO YOU STILL HAVE THAT BOOK I GAVE YOU? THE OMNIBUS! LOOK AT **PAGE 167!**
YEAH, YOU JUST DO SOME **READING** WHILE I CHOP YOU UP INTO LITTLE BITS.

ER, CHOPPING IS AGAINST THE RULES, RIGHT?
GO AHEAD, NATHAN, OPEN THE BOOK!

"MAX'S IMMOVABLE FORCE FIELD OF TOTAL INDESTRUCTABILITY"!

THIS WOULD PROBABLY BE REALLY USEFUL IF I **UNDERSTOOD** ANY OF IT.
MAX'S IMMOVABLE FORCE FIELD OF TOTAL INDESTRUCTIBILITY
WELL, WHEN I DID IT BEFORE, I JUST DREW OUT THE **RIGHT SYMBOLS.**
THAT MUST BE HOW THE STAFF WORKS, SO I'LL JUST COPY THE SYMBOLS ON THE PAGE!
SKRITCH SKRITCH

VOOM

UHHH...
IS THIS THING ON?

WELL, HERE GOES NOTHING.
YAAAH!

SWING

ACK!

DON'T GET *TOO FULL* OF YOURSELF. ALL I HAVE TO DO IS MAKE SURE YOU CAN'T MOVE...
...PAST ME?
RATTLE
WAIT A MINUTE!
I CAN'T MOVE!

WOW! INSTEAD OF PUTTING A BARRIER AROUND HIMSELF, HE PUT A BARRIER AROUND *ZACH!* BRILLIANT!
YEAAAH... JUST LIKE I PLANNED.

AAARGH!
DON'T YOU EVEN **THINK** ABOUT IT!
SCURRY

HEY, NEW GUY.
YOU DID PRETTY GOOD!
EVEN IF YOU ARE A
LITTLE BIT **CLUELESS.**
EHEH HEH HEH!
I'LL JUST TAKE
THAT AS A
COMPLIMENT.
YOINK!
SWIPE

WOW!
NICE!
GREAT!
BET YOU'LL
FIT RIGHT IN!
NOBODY LIKES
ZACH ANYWAY.
COME ON,
I'LL SHOW YOU
TO YOUR **NEXT**
CLASS!

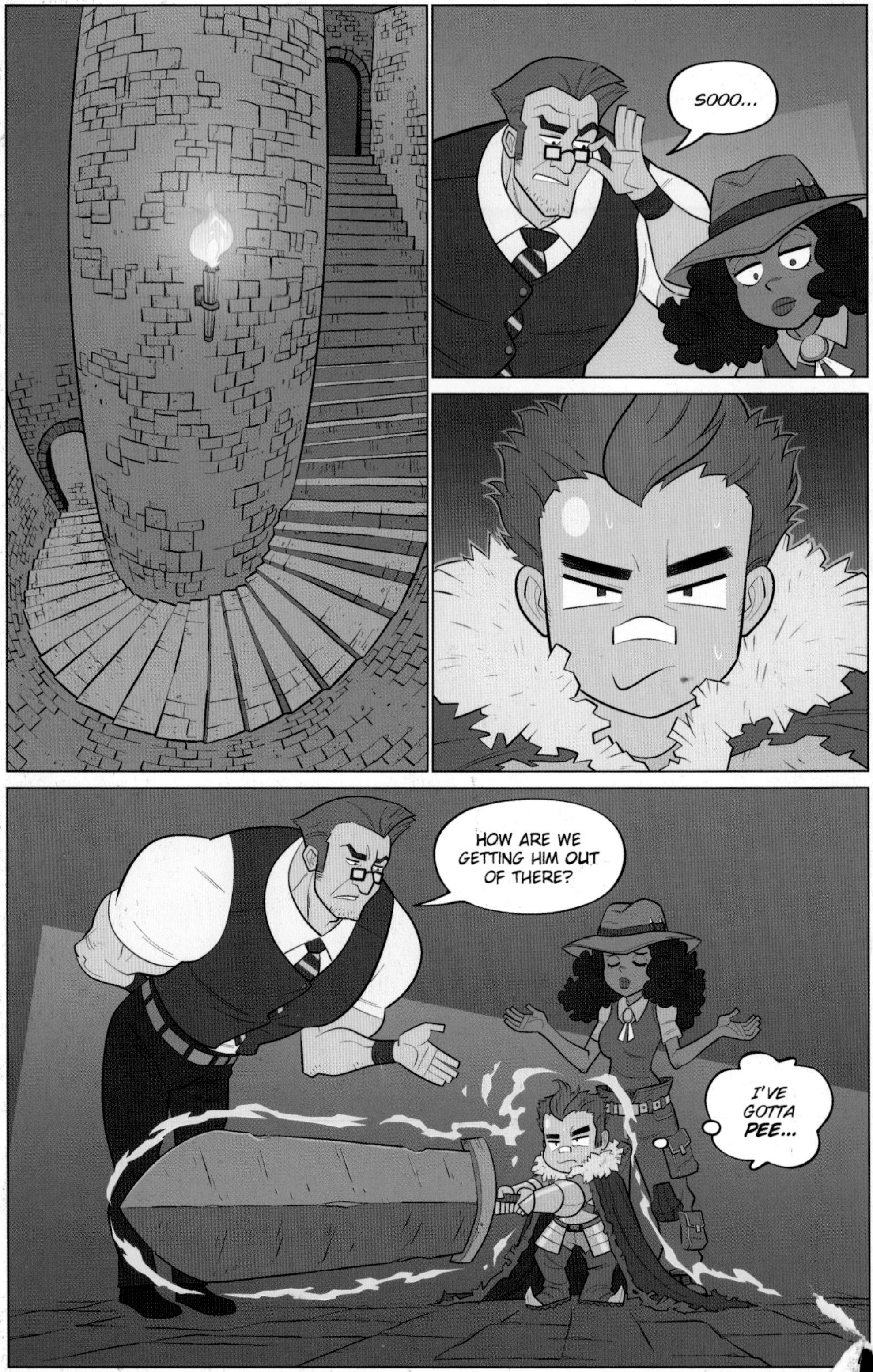

SOOO...

HOW ARE WE GETTING HIM OUT OF THERE?

I'VE GOTTA **PEE...**

CHAPTER THREE

WE'VE GOT A NEW STUDENT WITH US TODAY, SO I'D LIKE TO REVISIT A VERY BASIC QUESTION.

WHAT *IS* MAGIC?

WHEN I WAS YOUR AGE, **SCIENCE** WAS THE ONLY TOOL WE HAD TO UNDERSTAND THE UNIVERSE.

BUT SCIENCE CAN ONLY DESCRIBE THE LAWS OF NATURE.

FOOM

MAGIC **BREAKS** THOSE LAWS.

EARTH IS NOT A VERY MAGICAL PLACE. THE FURTHER AWAY FROM THE PORTAL YOU GET, THE *WEAKER* MAGIC BECOMES.

HERE AT THE SCHOOL WE'RE CLOSE ENOUGH THAT IT MAKES LITTLE DIFFERENCE, BUT DON'T FORGET: *THIS POWER COMES FROM ANOTHER WORLD.*

SIZZLE

THIS GUY'S TOO OLD TO HAVE EVER GONE ON ADVENTURES THROUGH THE PORTAL.

WHISPER

HOW'D HE LEARN TO CAST SPELLS?

WHISPER

HE NEVER SAYS, BUT HE *DEFINITELY* KNOWS HIS STUFF.

EACH OF YOU IS HERE BECAUSE YOU HAVE THE TALENT FOR MAGIC. SOME OF YOU HAVE **MORE** THAN OTHERS.
BUT IT'S NOT GOING TO BE EASY FOR ANY OF YOU TO LEARN WHAT YOU NEED TO KNOW TO **PROTECT** YOUR TEAMMATES ON THE OTHER SIDE.

AND FOR A LATE TRANSFER, IT'LL BE **EVEN HARDER.**
GULP!

NATHAN!
HUH? *WHA--?* ME?

LET'S SEE WHAT YOU'VE GOT. WHY DON'T YOU SHOW US A **SPELL?**

UH...WELL...I HAVEN'T EXACTLY *MEMORIZED* ONE OR ANYTHING...

DO ME A FAVOR AND TURN TO PAGE FIFTY-SIX IN YOUR OMNIBUS.
OH, SURE. JUST LET ME GET MY...
...BRICK?!
I HAD IT JUST FIFTEEN MINUTES AGO!

YOUR FIRST CLASS, AND YOU'RE ALREADY MAKING **EXCUSES?**
I'M SURE IT WAS IN HERE SOMEWHERE...!

SURE AM GLAD I DON'T NEED TO LEARN ANY OF THIS MUMBO-JUMBO!

YOU **LOST** YOUR TEXTBOOK.
THE *EXTREMELY IMPORTANT* ONE THAT I SPECIFICALLY ASKED ASHA TO GIVE YOU?
I GUESS I DID.

AND WHAT'S MORE, YOU DON'T KNOW HOW TO CAST EVEN A *SINGLE* SPELL.
I AM ACTUALLY REALLY GLAD SOMEBODY FINALLY NOTICED THAT.
TWIDDLE

DO YOU REALIZE WE'RE ONLY A **MONTH** AWAY FROM EVERYONE BEING PUT INTO A PORTAL TEAM?
YOU'VE GOT A LOT OF CATCHING UP TO DO.
I'M NOT GOING TO LET YOU JOIN THE FIRST EXPEDITION IF YOU'RE NOT READY.
I'LL WORK DOUBLE, *TRIPLE* HARD! I SWEAR!

OR MAYBE I COULD JUST **QUIT**...BUT THEN I CAN FORGET ABOUT BEING A HERO.

DON'T LOSE IT A SECOND TIME.
PLONK

SKRITCH SKRITCH
BE HONEST. HOW MANY **RUNES** DID YOU LEARN BEFORE YOU GOT HERE?
"RUNES"? ARE THOSE LIKE MAGIC WORDS?

YOU DON'T KNOW *ANY*?
NOT A SINGLE ONE.
EHEH!
POKE POKE

NOPE. NO WAY. THIS IS **HOPELESS.** THERE'S NO WAY I CAN GET YOU UP TO SNUFF IN TIME.
I'M SENDING YOU TO A **PRIVATE MAGIC TUTOR** FOR THE REST OF THE MONTH. THE VERY BEST WE HAVE.
DIDN'T YOU LITERALLY WRITE THE BOOK ON IT?

WHO DO YOU THINK I LEARNED FROM?

WELL, I *THINK* THIS IS THE PLACE...

UH... HELLO?
IT'S ME, NATHAN.
PROFESSOR DONENSTONE SENT ME.
SQUINT
KRAKOOM
EEK!

ER...

FOOM
FOOM
WHO DARES DEFILE MY SANCTUM?

AH...THE MORTAL CHILD. YOUR COMING WAS FORETOLD.

WH-WHO ARE YOU?
WHAT ARE YOU?!

A CREATURE OF AIR AND DARKNESS. A BEING OF MIST AND SHADOW.
I AM MAL'GHAST, THE MOST FIENDISH OF THE ELDAR, AND FROM THIS DAY ON, YOU WILL OBEY MY COMMANDS.

!

DASH

SLAM

BE SEATED, NATHAN GREENE.
I KNEW THIS HOUR WOULD COME.
SCREECH

YOU DID?
SCREEECH

I LEARNED BY **TEXT MESSAGE**. IT IS WRITTEN UPON THE SCREEN OF THIS ALL-SEEING EYE-PHONE.

YOU'RE NOT HUMAN!
YES, SO IT WOULD SEEM. DO TRY TO KEEP UP.
YOU'RE...YOU'RE A **VAMPIRE!** I'M WARNING YOU--

BWA HA HA HA HA!
HWOOOOOOOOO

S-SOMEBODY HELP?
A *VAMPIRE?* THE VERY IDEA!
DO YOU SEE ANY **FANGS** HERE?!

ALL RIGHT, ALL RIGHT! NOT A VAMPIRE. THE **GARLIC BREATH** PROVES IT!
I SEE IT IS NOT ONLY MAGIC WHERE YOUR EDUCATION IS LACKING. I AM NO MONSTER. I AM AN **ELF**.
A DARK ELF.

AN ELF. OKAY. 'CAUSE, YOU KNOW, ALL THE SKULLS AND SPIDERS KINDA GIVE THE WRONG IDEA.
THEY REMIND ME OF **HOME**.

SO YOU'RE MY NEW MAGIC TEACHER, HUH? A WEIRDO ELF!
I AM UNFAMILIAR WITH THIS "WEIRDO," BUT I SENSE IT TO BE A PEJORATIVE.

I HAVE NO IDEA WHAT THAT WORD MEANS.
I AM HERE TO TEACH YOU THE LANGUAGE OF THE ARCANE. WE HAVE ONE MONTH.
ARE YOU PREPARED TO GAZE INTO THE ABYSS OF MAGIC AND SEEK THE ELUSIVE FLAME OF WISDOM?
UHHH... I DON'T KNOW, ACTUALLY.

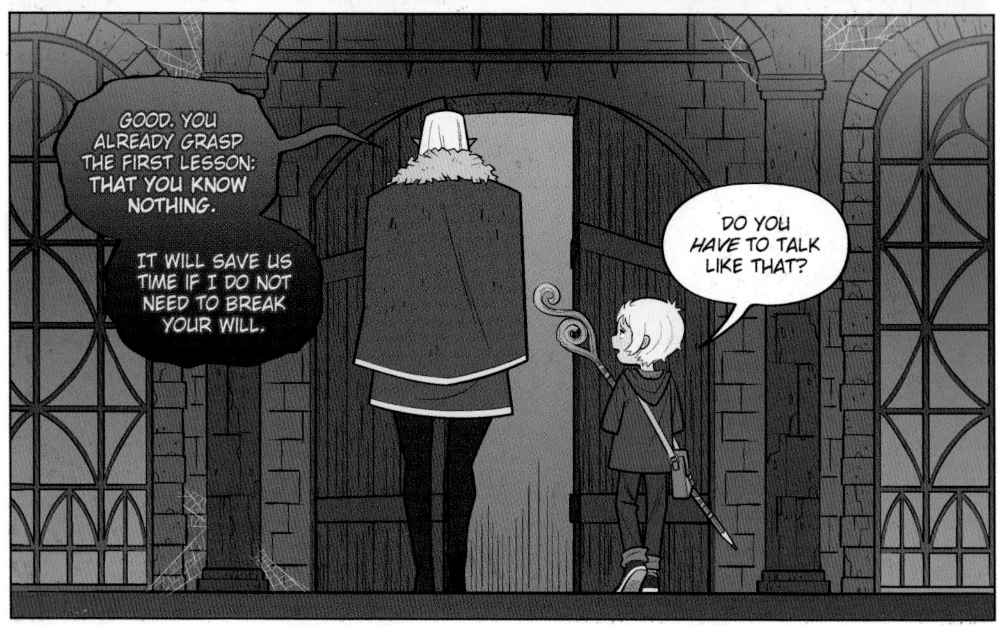
GOOD. YOU ALREADY GRASP THE FIRST LESSON: THAT YOU KNOW NOTHING.
IT WILL SAVE US TIME IF I DO NOT NEED TO BREAK YOUR WILL.
DO YOU HAVE TO TALK LIKE THAT?

SHUFFLE SHUFFLE

GROAN

OH, HEY. NEW KID. WHERE THE HECK HAVE YOU BEEN?
IN THE NASTIEST CATCH-UP CRAM SCHOOL EVER.

NO WAY! THEY STUCK YOU WITH THE ELF? NOBODY EVER SURVIVES THAT GUY'S PROGRAM!
I THOUGHT THEY STOPPED LETTING HIM TEACH CLASSES!

THE FORGE

HE'S PRETTY INTENSE... BUT HE *IS* AN ELF, AND ISN'T THAT AWESOME? THAT'S LIKE AS **FANTASY** AS IT GETS!

YEAH, BUT KEEP QUIET ABOUT IT. THEY DON'T THINK THE WHOLE WORLD'S READY TO LEARN ABOUT ELVES JUST YET.

HE TOLD ME THAT THE ACADEMY RESCUED HIM FROM THE DUNGEON. THAT'S SO COOL!

YUP. AND SOMEDAY, I'M GOING TO RESCUE AN **ELVEN PRINCESS** AND MAKE HER MY **BRIDE.**

HMM. EVEN GEEKY-LOOKING GUYS LIKE US NEED **DREAMS.**

EXCUSE ME?

MY SKIN'S ALREADY CLEARING UP, OKAY?!
I DIDN'T MEAN IT LIKE--
I'M **DUNCAN DONALDSON**, THE GREAT MAGICIAN. REMEMBER THE NAME!
IT'S GOING TO BE LEGENDARY! IN ALL THE WORLDS! SO DON'T SNARK AT ME ABOUT MY DREAMS!
UH... OKAY...
THIS IS AWKWARD...

HEY, YOU'RE HERE TO VISIT THE **ARMORER**, TOO, RIGHT? THEY TOLD ME TO COME AND GRAB MY ADVENTURING GEAR, BUT I DON'T SEE HIM ANY--

CLANG

"GRAB," HE SAYS, LIKE EVERYTHING I MAKE ISN'T A CUSTOM, MADE-TO-ORDER MASTERPIECE!

TORQ'S THE NAME! **GEAR'S** THE GAME.

I MAKE ALL THE WEAPONS AND ARMOR FOR OUR STUDENTS AND NEVER ONCE SERVED THEM WRONG.

WOW! YOU'RE A DWARF.

LIKE A REAL, GIMLI-STYLE DWARF.

I RECKON YOU AIN'T DONE GROWING YET... GOING TO NEED A BIT **EXTRA** THROUGH THE SHOULDERS TO ALLOW FOR THAT...

MAGE, SO NOT TOO HEAVY... RIGHT, RIGHT, RIGHT.

THOUGH, I'VE GOT A **TIP** FOR YOU, KIDDO.

CLICK

YEAH?

QUIT THE MAGIC GAME! GET INTO **SCIENCE**. IT'S A MAGIC ANYONE CAN DO.
HOO *HOO!* A **GAMER,** I SEE! AND YOU GOT THE LIMITED EDITION FACEPLATE AND EVERYTHING! WHO NEEDS WIZARDRY WHEN YOU GOT GIZMOS LIKE THIS?
WHOA, EASY!
I BOUGHT THAT WITH MY OWN MONEY, YOU KNOW.
SLAP

SO, *UH,* WELCOME TO EARTH, I GUESS.
IT'S THE PLACE I WAS ALWAYS **MEANT** TO BE!
A FEW SIPS OF BOXED JUICE, THEN I'LL MAKE YOU LOOK A RIGHT PROPER **MAGE,** IF THAT'S WHAT YOU WANT, LAD.
SLURRRRP...

THAT'D BE GREAT. JUST MAYBE A LITTLE LESS...*EVERYTHING*... THAN HIS OUTFIT.
SAY NO MORE.
SIP SIP...

BWISH

HUH. WELL, IT SURE FEELS LIKE I'M READY FOR ANOTHER WORLD.
THE FEELING IS HALF THE BATTLE! WHAT'S MORE, THE SPECIAL FIBERS IN THAT GETUP CAN RESIST BOTH FANG AND STEEL.

SHOULD WE MAYBE TEST THAT OUT?
DRAAAG

HEY, ZACH. SORRY ABOUT THE WHOLE, UH, TRAPPING-YOU-IN-A-BUBBLE THING.
NICE TIGHTS, ZELDA.

NO, UH, COMMON MISCONCEPTION. ZELDA'S THE PRINCESS, ACTUALLY. THE HERO IS--

I PLAYED THE GAME TOO, "ZELDA."
HAR! HAR!
YOU KIDS PLAY NICE, NOW!

ARE YOU AND ME REALLY GOING TO BE LIKE THIS, OR CAN WE JUST BE FRIENDS INSTEAD?
WHATEVER YOU WANNA CALL IT. I'LL BE STRAIGHT WITH YOU, THOUGH. MOST OF US HERE ARE RISK-TAKERS, AND YOU KIND OF SEEM LIKE A WIMP.
REMINDS ME OF MY OLD PARTNER.
HE DIDN'T WANT TO DO WHAT IT TAKES TO BE AN ADVENTURER, NOT REALLY. HE JUST KIND OF LIKED THE IDEA OF BEING SPECIAL.

WHAT'S SPECIAL IS YOUR TASTE IN BLADES. WHAT'S THIS EVEN SUPPOSED TO BE?

TAKE IT FROM A DWARF, LAD. BIGGER IS NOT ALWAYS BETTER.
WHAT'S THAT SUPPOSED TO MEAN?!
GRIP

LISTEN. I'VE LIVED MY WHOLE LIFE WATCHING PEOPLE COOLER THAN ME TALK ABOUT THEIR ADVENTURES OR THEIR GIRLFRIENDS OR THEIR VACATIONS TO FIJI OR WHATEVER, AND ALL I EVER DID WAS SIT AT HOME AND DRAW AND PLAY VIDEO GAMES.
I'M HERE TO DO SOMETHING THAT MATTERS.

HMMM...
HOW QUAINT.
ACK!

THERE IS NO TIME FOR SUCH CHIT-CHAT.
WE HAVE WORK TO DO.
ERR... I WAS JUST FINISHING UP, MR. MAL'GHAST, SIR...!

YOUR ERRAND IS COMPLETE.
AND THERE ARE SEVEN-HUNDRED-AND-FIFTY-TWO RUNES LEFT TO MEMORIZE, IF YOU ARE TO HAVE ANY HOPE OF JOINING THE EXPEDITION.
SNAP
GRUUU!

HOO HOO! GOOD LUCK, LAD. YOU'LL NEED IT!
GRUUUUUU...

SO, YOU SURVIVED MAL'S TRAINING.

GROAN...
THAT GUY IS **RELENTLESS!**
UGH!
NO ONE ELSE COULD TEACH YOU THE BASICS SO QUICKLY.

I THINK I COULD WRITE ALL THE RUNES THAT EVER EXISTED BACKWARDS AND FORWARDS IN MY SLEEP.
DON'T EVEN GET ME STARTED ON **INCANTATIONS!**
WRING
I'M AN **ARTIST**, I TOLD HIM, "I DON'T CHANT!" BUT HE INSISTED.
SHOW ME WHAT YOU'VE LEARNED.
FWOP

SO, I START WITH AN EMPTY CIRCLE.
SHFF

SKRITCH
AROUND THE OUTSIDE, I SCRIBBLE WHERE I WANT THE SPELL TO **GO...**

AND ON THE INSIDE, I PUT IN WHAT I WANT IT TO ***DO.***
THE MORE COMPLICATED THE **SPELL,** THE MORE RUNES I HAVE TO USE.
SKRITCH

WE TRIED A WHOLE LOT OF SPELLS, AND CAME UP WITH A HANDFUL I CAN DO RELIABLY.
YOU'RE STILL A BEGINNER.
A LOT OF THE SPELLS ARE BOUND TO BE TOO HARD FOR YOU JUST YET.

AND WHEN I'M DONE, I **CLOSE** THE CIRCLE TO COMPLETE THE SPELL.
TAK

VOOM

HMM... LEVITATION. NOT BAD.

BUT THERE IS ONE BIG PROBLEM.

EVEN SO, GOING FROM ZERO MAGIC TO *ANY* MAGIC IS LIKE AN INFINITE PERCENT IMPROVEMENT!

HOW MANY SPELLS CAN I DO?
THREE AT BEST. NEVER TRY FOR FOUR, NATHAN, OR YOU MIGHT PASS OUT FOR **DAYS,** OR WORSE.

BUT YOU THINK THIS GETS ME CAUGHT UP?

WELL, IT'S NOT IDEAL... BUT IT'S THE MOST WE COULD HOPE FOR IN A **MONTH,** AND YOU DO HAVE A VERY POWERFUL STAFF ON YOUR SIDE.
I'LL TELL PRINCIPAL WALKER THAT YOU'RE READY TO JOIN THE EXPEDITION.
CAN I PLEASE SWAP BACK TO **NORMAL CLASSES** NOW?

AND HERE I THOUGHT YOU'D TRULY **ENJOYED** OUR TIME TOGETHER.
DO YOU HAVE TO KEEP *DOING* THAT?!

THIS TIME TOMORROW, ALL OF YOU ARE GOING TO WALK THROUGH THIS **GATE.**

FOR MOST OF YOU, IT'LL BE THE **FIRST TIME.**

WHAT WE'VE LEARNED OVER THE YEARS IS THAT IT'S BEST TO SEND STUDENTS IN GROUPS OF **THREE.**
MORE THAN THAT, AND IT GETS HARD TO MANEUVER IN TIGHT HALLWAYS. LESS THAN THAT, AND YOU DON'T HAVE ALL THE **SKILLS** YOU NEED. EACH GROUP NEEDS A BALANCE OF SPECIALISTS.

YOU'VE PROBABLY HEARD, BUT THE SHORTHAND WE USE IS **FIGHTER, MAGE,** AND **THIEF.**
NOD NOD

WE *REALLY* NEED TO CALL THIEF SOMETHING ELSE...
YOU KNOW, YOU SAID THAT BACK WHEN *I* WAS A FRESHMAN.

ANYWAY, MOST OF YOU ALREADY HAVE YOUR TEAMS.
EVERYBODY WITH A FULL GROUP, PLEASE STAND OVER HERE.

YEAH, I GUESS BEING ON HER TEAM WAS TOO MUCH TO HOPE FOR.
CAN'T PUT TWO MAGIC USERS IN THE SAME GROUP, SEEMS LIKE.

OH, CRIPES. BIGSWORD McSHORTSTUFF OVER THERE IS A SOLO, TOO.
DEFINITELY DON'T WANT TO PARTNER WITH HIM.
DON'T MAKE EYE CONTACT!
DON'T MAKE EYE CONTACT!
HMMM...
PICK PICK

MANDY, I'D LIKE FOR YOU TO GROUP UP WITH ZACH.
EXCUSE ME?!
YOU'RE NOT MUCH FOR FIGHTING, AND HE'S NOT MUCH FOR BOOK SMARTS. YOU'LL BE A PERFECT BALANCE.

UGH!
EWW!
NO WAY! YOU HAVE TO BE JOKING. YOU'RE GOING TO TURN ME INTO THIS BRAT'S **BABYSITTER?!**
FLICK

HMMN... THOSE TWO LOOK A LOT MORE DANGEROUS, THAT'S FOR SURE. WOULDN'T THEY BE A BETTER BET?
I'D LIKE TO TEAM UP WITH--
WHAP

I'LL TAKE MANDY, BUT *ONLY* IF I CAN HAVE NATHAN.
WAIT, WHAT?
IF YOU SURVIVED THAT OLD ELF'S TRAINING, YOU CAN SURVIVE ANYTHING. AND AFTER MY LAST PARTNER, I WANT A TEAM OF **SURVIVORS.**

WELL, I'D ACTUALLY RATHER GO WITH--
OH, VERY WELL. I SUPPOSE I SHALL ALLOW YOU TO JOIN ME, DUNCAN.

GREAT! THEN THAT'S EVERYONE IN A TEAM. ZACH, IT'S NICE TO SEE YOU GETTING ALONG WITH SOMEONE FOR A CHANGE.
WELL THEN, MAKE ME **PROUD**, KIDS!

WELCOME ABOARD, BUDDY.
AND DON'T THINK FOR A SECOND I'VE FORGOTTEN ABOUT WHAT YOU *DID TO ME* IN THE MAZE.
TWITCH TWITCH
PAT PAT
THIS COULDN'T POSSIBLY BE WORSE!

CHAPTER FOUR

THE DAY OF THE FIRST EXPEDITION.

THIS IS IT.
THIS IS THE DAY
YOU'VE ALL BEEN
WAITING FOR!

ON THE OTHER SIDE OF THIS GATE, THERE'S A WORLD OF **ADVENTURE** WAITING FOR YOU.
BUT IT'S ALSO A WORLD OF **DANGER!**
BECAUSE OF THAT DANGER, YOU'LL ALL HAVE A **MENTOR** FROM OUR SENIOR CLASS.
FOLLOW THEIR INSTRUCTIONS *TO THE LETTER.*

I DON'T NEED TO REMIND YOU THAT THE TRAPS AND MONSTERS IN THERE ARE **DEADLY.**
EACH OF YOU HAS BEEN ASSIGNED AN UNEXPLORED REGION TO INVESTIGATE.
YOU'LL HAVE **SIX HOURS** TO EXPLORE, AND WHILE YOU'RE AT IT, RETRIEVE ANY **ARTIFACTS** YOU MIGHT HAPPEN TO FIND.

BUT IT'S NOT JUST TREASURE I WANT YOU LOOKING FOR!
WHETHER IT'S ANCIENT KNOWLEDGE OR YOUR OWN HAND-DRAWN MAPS, EVERY DISCOVERY YOU MAKE WILL HELP YOU MOVE **UP** IN THE CLASS RANKINGS.
SOMEWHERE OUT THERE, **THE TRUTH** IS WAITING.

AND MORE IMPORTANTLY, THE *TREASURE* IS WAITING!
JUST KEEP YOUR STICKY FINGERS **OUT** OF MY POCKETS.
COME ON, YOU TWO, LET'S BE SERIOUS!
GRRR!

SHOOOM

ENTER, IF THOU ART WORTHY.

HEY, KID. LONG TIME NO SEE.
YOU READY?
I SURE HOPE SO.
YOU GOT NOTHING TO WORRY ABOUT. WE'VE GOT *TWO* DRAGONSLAYERS ON THIS TEAM!
HEH!

CLOP
WHOA.
THIS PLACE IS HUGE!

LOOKS LIKE EVERYONE ELSE ALREADY MOVED ON AHEAD...
SO. WELCOME TO **THE NEXUS.**

WHAT IS IT?
YOU MUST NOT KNOW, SINCE YOU'RE THE NEW GUY AND MAYBE KIND OF DUMB.
THE NEXUS IS A KIND OF **STAGING AREA.** YOU CAN GET TO ANY PART OF THE DUNGEON FROM HERE, *IF* YOU KNOW THE RIGHT PATH.

TOILET
HEY, BATHROOMS! HOW CONVENIENT.
IT'S REALLY, *REALLY* EASY TO LOSE YOUR WAY. MORE THAN ONE CARELESS ADVENTURER HAS GONE MISSING AND NEVER RETURNED!
A TERRIBLE MONSTER COULD LURK BEHIND EVERY DOOR!

TOILET
CREAK

UH, NEVER MIND.
WRIGGLE

ZIP

UH, GUYS?
HELLO?
UH-OH.

EEEEEP!

DIDN'T YOU HEAR ME? DON'T FALL BEHIND!
THIS PLACE ISN'T KIDDING AROUND.
HAVEN'T YOU SEEN THE BLEACHED BONES?
I SURE HAVE NOW...

WEREN'T THERE SUPPOSED TO BE MOUNTAINS OF TREASURE IN HERE?
LONG GONE, DUH! HOW DO YOU THINK THEY PAID FOR THE SCHOOL? A GOOD THIEF NEVER LETS TREASURE GO TO WASTE!

BEFORE
AFTER

YOU KNOW, SPEAKING OF THIEVERY, NOW THAT I'M LOOKING AT IT...
YOUR OUTFIT...
DOESN'T LOOK VERY SNEAKY.
RULE NUMBER ONE OF BEING A THIEF: *NEVER* DRESS LIKE A THIEF!
WHICH RULE IS THE ONE THAT TELLS YOU TO DRESS LIKE A **CLOWN?**
HEH HEH!

HMPH!
RULE NUMBER TWO: YOU CAN'T BE FAMOUS IF YOU DON'T CUT A **FLASHY FIGURE!**

BESIDES, WHEN STUFF GOES MISSING, WHO DO YOU THINK THE MONSTERS'LL COME AFTER FIRST: THE SCOWLY GUY WITH THE SWORD OR A SWEET, INNOCENT GIRL LIKE ME?
TEE HEE HEE!

DID YOU ALL REMEMBER TO BRING YOUR MAPS?
THERE WAS A **MAP**?
A-ARE WE LOST?
OOH! OOH! I'VE GOT MINE!

LIKE CYRUS SAID, WE'VE GOT OUR OWN EXPLORATION TARGET. IT'S IN A REGION I KNOW ESPECIALLY WELL.

MOST OF THE ARTIFACTS NEARBY ALREADY GOT CLEARED OUT. SO IF WE WANT TO FIND ANY, WE NEED TO HEAD **DEEPER** INSIDE.
SO WHAT KIND OF PLACE ARE WE HEADED TO...?

IT'S CALLED **THE GREAT SUBTERRANE.** IT'S A PRACTICALLY ENDLESS MESS OF CAVES, TUNNELS, AND RUINED VAULTS AT THE LOWEST LEVEL OF THE DUNGEON.
FROM WHAT I HEARD IN CLASS, WE CAN PROBABLY PASS THROUGH UNNOTICED. THE MONSTERS THERE FIGHT *EACH OTHER* MORE THAN THEY FIGHT VISITORS.

ABOVE THAT IS **THE GOLDEN PLAIN,** A CAVE SO BIG IT HAS ITS OWN GRASSY FIELDS AND ARTIFICIAL SUN.

OUTSIDE IS **THE KING'S QUARTER,** A CASTLE THAT'S NEVER STOPPED GROWING, BECAUSE THE GOLEM BUILDERS HAVE KEPT ADDING MORE AND MORE ROOMS, EVEN ALL THESE AGES AFTER THE ORIGINAL OWNERS LEFT.

TAP TAP

THE SCARLET SPIRES.

WHAT'S OVER THERE?

LOTS OF PEOPLE HAVE TRIED TO MAKE IT. *NO ONE'S* EVER PULLED IT OFF.
FOLD
TUSSLE
HNGH!
GRRR!
I USED TO DREAM OF BEING THE FIRST.

WELL, YOU'VE STILL GOT **TIME**, RIGHT?
HUMPH!

THE TUNNELS ARE AT THE BOTTOM OF THE STAIRS.
COME ON, WE GOT A LOT OF **WALKING** TO DO.

THIS THING IS **IMPOSSIBLE** TO FOLD UP! COULDN'T THEY JUST MAKE THE MAP INTO AN ***APP*** OR SOMETHING?
YEAH, RIGHT. YOU KNOW AS WELL AS ME THAT TECHNOLOGY IS **WORTHLESS** HERE.

NOD

STEP

SHWOOOOO

UHHHHH...

THWAP
BLEACHED BONES, NATHAN!
BLEACHED BONES!
OUCH!

IF YOU GET LOST AGAIN, I SWEAR I'M ***NOT*** COMING BACK FOR YOU!
OH, COME ON, WAIT UP!

C'MON, GUYS, SLOW DOWN.

NO WAY! TREASURE AWAITS!

EEEEK!

CRUMBLE

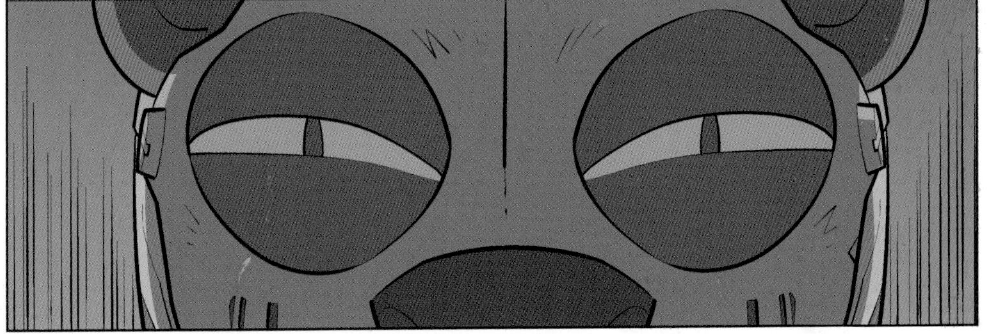

JUST MY IMAGINATION! DEFINITELY **JUST** MY IMAGINATION!

Hey, numbskull!
Wakey-wakey!

Come, come!
Lookie-lookie!
Eh? *Eh?*
Whuzzat?

Humans!
Oh, no!
We gotsta tell
the boss!

Down in Goblin Town...

THE MOST FEARSOME... THE MOST LOATHSOME... THE MOST *HORRIBLE* GOBLIN OF ALL...

THE LORD OF GOBLINS COMETH!

BOW DOWN, WORMS!

FOR AN AGE, MY LORD GOBBINGTON, YOUR BLOODLINE HAS LED THE GOBLIN TRIBES FROM VICTORY TO VICTORY.

WE CONQUERED THE KOBOLDS. WE COMMAND THE TUNNELS. WE *SEIZED* THIS MIGHTY CASTLE!

I'M PRETTY **AWESOME**, IT'S TRUE.

NOW MORE THAN EVER, WE NEED YOUR **LEADERSHIP**. DREADFUL, WRETCHED CREATURES HAVE COME UPON OUR LANDS!

WAIT, WHAT?

Humans, master! Human intruders!!
They had big, scary, pointy swords!
HUMANS? N-NONSENSE. THERE HASN'T BEEN A HUMAN IN OUR PART OF THE DUNGEON FOR AGES!

DISGUSTING HUMAN!
UGLY HUMAN!
TASTY HUMAN!

The mightiest goblin warriors.

THEY'RE REALLY THE BEST WE'VE GOT?

IT *HAS* BEEN A WHILE SINCE THE LAST WAR AGAINST THE ELVES, YOUR MAJESTY.

GET THESE **LOSERS** OUT OF HERE.

The craftiest goblin beastmasters.

WOOF! WOOF!

WHAT KIND OF **TRAINING** WERE YOU **DOING**, EXACTLY?!
THEY ALSO KNOW HOW TO ROLL OVER!
DING-A-LING
PANT! PANT!
NEXT!

The evilest and darkest necrogoblins.

NOW **THAT'S** MORE LIKE IT! THESE LOOK LIKE SOME REALLY NASTY GOBS WHO CAN GET RESULTS!

SOON WE WILL DRINK HUMAN BLOOD FROM *HUMAN SKULLS.*

YIKES! WHERE DID YOU FIND THESE GUYS?

THEY FOUND ME.

WHEN THE TIME COMES, YOU WILL SEE OUR *POWER.*

ALL RIGHT, YOU THREE. THIS IS WHERE THE MAP ENDS.
ON THE OTHER SIDE OF THIS DOOR IS A TOTALLY UNEXPLORED BRANCH OF THE DUNGEON.
OOH! AND BEHIND EVERY DOOR, SOMEWHERE, THERE'S AN **ARTIFACT** WAITING TO BE FOUND!

AND **MONSTERS.**
GOOD LUCK. I'LL BE WAITING RIGHT HERE.
WAIT...YOU'RE NOT COMING WITH US?

ALL PART OF THE PLAN.
IF YOU'RE NOT BACK IN A FEW HOURS, I'LL COME LOOKING FOR YOU.
ARE YOU SURE? IS IT **SAFE** IN THERE? WHAT'S IT LIKE? OH MAN, OH MAN...
DON'T WORRY, KID! IT'LL BE *FINE.* THERE WON'T BE MORE THAN A COUPLE WEAK MONSTERS AT WORST.

WITH ME, GOBBOS!
EVERY LAST ONE OF US RIDES TO WAR!

CHAPTER FIVE

THIS WAY!
THIS WAY!

HISS!

CREEPY.

SO, UH...
WE KNOW ANYTHING
ABOUT THIS PLACE?
DANGEROUS.
SMELLY.
UNFRIENDLY.

OVER HERE!
HURRY UP,
GUYS!

LOOKS LIKE MONSTER TERRITORY.

WHICH MEANS WE'RE GOING THROUGH THIS OTHER, NICER, *LESS* SKULL-DECORATED TUNNEL, RIGHT?

LUCKY FOR YOU, I ACTUALLY GO TO CLASS.
THIS IS THE LANGUAGE OF THE ANCIENT DUNGEON BUILDERS.
I DEFINITELY CAN'T READ IT EITHER.

I'LL SPELL IT OUT FOR YOU IN VERY SIMPLE WORDS. THIS INSCRIPTION SAYS...

HMMM...
WELL...I CAN'T READ IT PERFECTLY...

BUT IT SAYS THIS PLACE IS A **TREASURE VAULT!**

REALLY?
A TREASURE VAULT...
TALK ABOUT ***LUCK!*** WE'VE GOTTA RISK IT!
IF WE FIND A WHOLE TREASURE VAULT ON OUR FIRST TRIP, OUR RANK IS **GUARANTEED** TO SHOOT RIGHT UP TO FIRST PLACE!
STROKE STROKE

I'D RATHER BE AN ALIVE LAST PLACE THAN A *DEAD* FIRST PLACE.
DON'T BE A WUSS. WE TRAINED FOR THIS!
SOME OF US LONGER THAN OTHERS, I'LL REMIND YOU!

LOOKS LIKE A DEAD END.

ZACH, YOU REALLY SHOULDN'T RUN AHEAD LIKE THAT! I SHOULD BE THE ONE IN FRONT.

YEAH? AND WHAT ARE YOU GOING TO DO IF YOU WALK INTO A MONSTER? HIDE BEHIND *ME*, I BET.
YEAH? AND WHAT ARE YOU GOING TO DO IF YOU STOMP RIGHT INTO A **TRAP?!**

UH, GUYS?
Well...this is awkward.

HEH
HEH
HEH!

THE HUMANS!

HUMANS!

KILL THE HUMANS!

REAL NICE WORK, ZACH...

WE ARE SO BUSTED.

WE DID IT!!
WHAP
I NEVER THOUGHT WE'D FIND AN **ARTIFACT** ON OUR FIRST ADVENTURE.
OOH, SPARKLY.
MAKES ME WONDER HOW THE THREE **REJECTS** ARE DOING.
REJECTS?

DON'T PLAY DUMB. THE IDIOTS! THE JERKS! THE LOSERS!
SNAP
OH, YOU MEAN **ZACH.**
YOU BET I DO! DO YOU KNOW HOW HE RANKS IN TEAMWORK? **DEAD LAST.** IN BOOK SMARTS? **DEAD LAST.** EVERY SINGLE CHANCE HE GETS, HE RUINS THINGS FOR EVERYONE!
LIKE THAT TIME HE SNUCK INTO THE PORTAL WITHOUT PERMISSION...
HE DRAGGED ALONG HIS OLD PARTNERS, TOO.
THEY WERE SO INJURED, *SO TERRIFIED*, THAT THEY DROPPED OUT OF SCHOOL AND **NEVER** CAME BACK!
BWA HA HA HA!

THAT'S HOW HE GOT HIS SWORD!
AN UNBREAKABLE EVIL WEAPON THAT ENDLESSLY CALLS OUT FOR...
HUMAN BLOOD!

I DON'T KNOW ABOUT *THAT.*

HIS NEW PARTNERS? THEY'RE DOOMED!
DOOMED, I TELL YOU!

KILL THE HUMANS!!
KILL THE HUMANS!!
KILL THE HUMANS!!

OH MAN, OH MAN, OH MAN... **WHAT DO WE DO?!**
RUN...?
HOW ARE WE SUPPOSED TO RUN WHEN THERE'S ***NO BRIDGE?!***
I *KNEW* I SHOULD HAVE BROUGHT A ROPE.

KE KE KE
HEH!

WHAM

WAIT, ZACH! YOUR SWORD'S SUPPOSED TO BE **UNBREAKABLE,** RIGHT?!
HEH HEH!
GUESS WE'RE ABOUT TO FIND OUT.

NO, *NO*--LAY IT OVER THE **EDGE!** IT'S JUST LONG ENOUGH TO WORK!
YOU'VE GOTTA BE KIDDING ME!
KILL! KILL!

CLANK

IT'S WORKING! IT'S WORKING!
HURRY! *QUICKLY!*
THONK
DON'T CROWD ME!

FLING
WHUD
TOSS
UGH! IT'S SO HEAVY!

COME ON, COME ON! WE'VE GOTTA RUN!

NO, WAIT. I'VE GOT THIS. I ONLY NEED LIKE TEN SECONDS!
SKRITCH
SKRITCH

VOOM
OKAY! TAKE COVER!!
ARE YOU TRYING TO HELP US ***OR KILL US?!***

BOOM

EEEE!
WHOA.

CRUMBLE

HEY, IT WORKED!
YOINK

NOT BAD, ZELDA! I'D LIKE TO SEE THEM TRY AND JUMP ACROSS THAT!
LESS TALKING, MORE RUNNING!

DID YOU SEE ME?

I WAS AWESOME!

I-IT WOULD APPEAR THE HUMANS HAVE **ESCAPED,** SIRE.

YEAH, BECAUSE *SOMEONE* THOUGHT WE SHOULD SEND IN A KOBOLD FIRST.
WHAP
FORGIVE YOUR UNWORTHY SERVANT, MY LIEGE!
WHATEVER. I'M PRETTY SURE I KNOW WHERE THEY'RE GOING.
TRULY? YOU ARE INDEED THE **WISEST** OF ALL GOBLINS!

IF THEY'RE HERE, IT MEANS ONLY ONE THING: THEY'RE HUNTING FOR OUR ANCIENT **TREASURE VAULT.**

THEY WOULD *DARE!*
EASY FIX. YOU THREE!
HOW MAY WE SERVE?

THERE'S A **SECRET SHORTCUT** TO THE VAULT.
IT'S TOO BIG FOR THE WHOLE ARMY, BUT I WANT YOU THREE FREAKSHOWS TO GO AHEAD AND GET A **SURPRISE** READY...

ZZZ...
ZZZ...

PANT!
PANT!
DOESN'T SOUND LIKE...THE GOBLINS ARE STILL FOLLOWING...
PANT!
WE DEFINITELY LOST THEM.

YEAH, BUT WHAT ABOUT *US*? ARE WE LOST?
HOW ARE WE SUPPOSED TO GET BACK?
LET'S WORRY ABOUT THE MINOR DETAILS *AFTER* WE GET THE TREASURE.

THERE ARE A SUSPICIOUSLY LARGE NUMBER OF **SKELETONS** AROUND HERE.
SKELETONS USUALLY MEAN EXACTLY ONE THING--
HOLD IT.

BUT, HEY, I SEE THIS AS GOOD NEWS!

WE *MUST* BE ON THE PATH TO THE VAULT, IF THEY'VE GOT STUFF LIKE ***THIS*** SET UP!

SWISH

FWIP

THUNK

BWOOSH

BUZZ

CRUMBLE

OKAY, OKAY! ZACH? DO NOT. DO **NOT** LIFT UP YOUR FOOT!

ST-STAY CALM! I THINK I SAW SOMETHING LIKE THIS IN A MOVIE.

IF WE PUT SOMETHING **HEAVY** IN THE PLACE OF HIS FOOT, WE'LL BE OKAY!

OH! I'VE GOT JUST THE THING.

THIS **DUMB BOOK** SHOULD WORK. IT'S AS HEAVY AS A **BRICK!**

THWAP

WHOA, WHOA, **WHOA!**

WHERE DID YOU GET THAT?
FOUND IT, I GUESS?

WHERE, EXACTLY?
IN YOUR POCKET, MAYBE...?
YOU *STOLE* MY SPELLBOOK?

I WAS GOING TO GIVE IT BACK WHEN I WAS DONE READING IT!
DO YOU REALIZE HOW MUCH **TROUBLE** I GOT INTO BECAUSE IT WAS MISSING?
HEY, PEOPLE. PRIORITIES?

WHY DON'T WE USE YOUR **SWORD?** IT'S PRETTY HEAVY.
ARE YOU KIDDING? DO YOU KNOW HOW MUCH TROUBLE I WENT THROUGH TO *GET* THIS THING?

THIS IS JUST GREAT! AT THIS RATE, WE'LL END UP LIKE ALL THESE DUMB SKELETONS OVER HERE.
THAT'S IT!
WHAT'S WHAT?

SKELETONS!
A WHAT NOW?
EH?

GREAT! PILING THEM UP LIKE THIS WAS PERFECT.
WE'RE **SQUARE** NOW, OKAY?
I'M *NOT* TOUCHING ANY MORE GROSS OLD BONES!
I DON'T SEE HOW THIS HELPS US, EXACTLY!
VOOM

HEY, WHAT ARE YOU TRYING TO PULL HERE?!
IS ONE OF THEM *DRIPPING*? **YUCK!**
OKAY, ZACH. ON THREE, I WANT YOU TO **ROLL** OUT OF THE WAY!

ONE...
YOU BETTER NOT SCREW THIS UP!
TWO...
BECAUSE IF YOU DO...
THREE!

ROLL
THUNK

HEH HEH! NICE!
SO, *NOW* DO YOU AGREE THE THIEF SHOULD TAKE THE LEAD?
BE MY GUEST.

ALL RIGHT, PEOPLE! LET'S FIND OUR **TREASURE!**
WE ARE DEFINITELY TALKING ABOUT THIS LATER!
TREASURE! TREASURE! *LA LA LA~!*

THINK WE CAN EAT IT?
WITH MUSHROOMS, THE SAFE ANSWER IS ALWAYS "NO."
THIS HAS **GOT** TO BE THE PLACE. WE NEVER PRACTICED WITH LOCKS *THIS TRICKY* IN CLASS...
CLICK
CLICK
KA-CHAK
NICE! GO, MANDY!
OH, THAT WAS PRETTY FA--
MMPH!

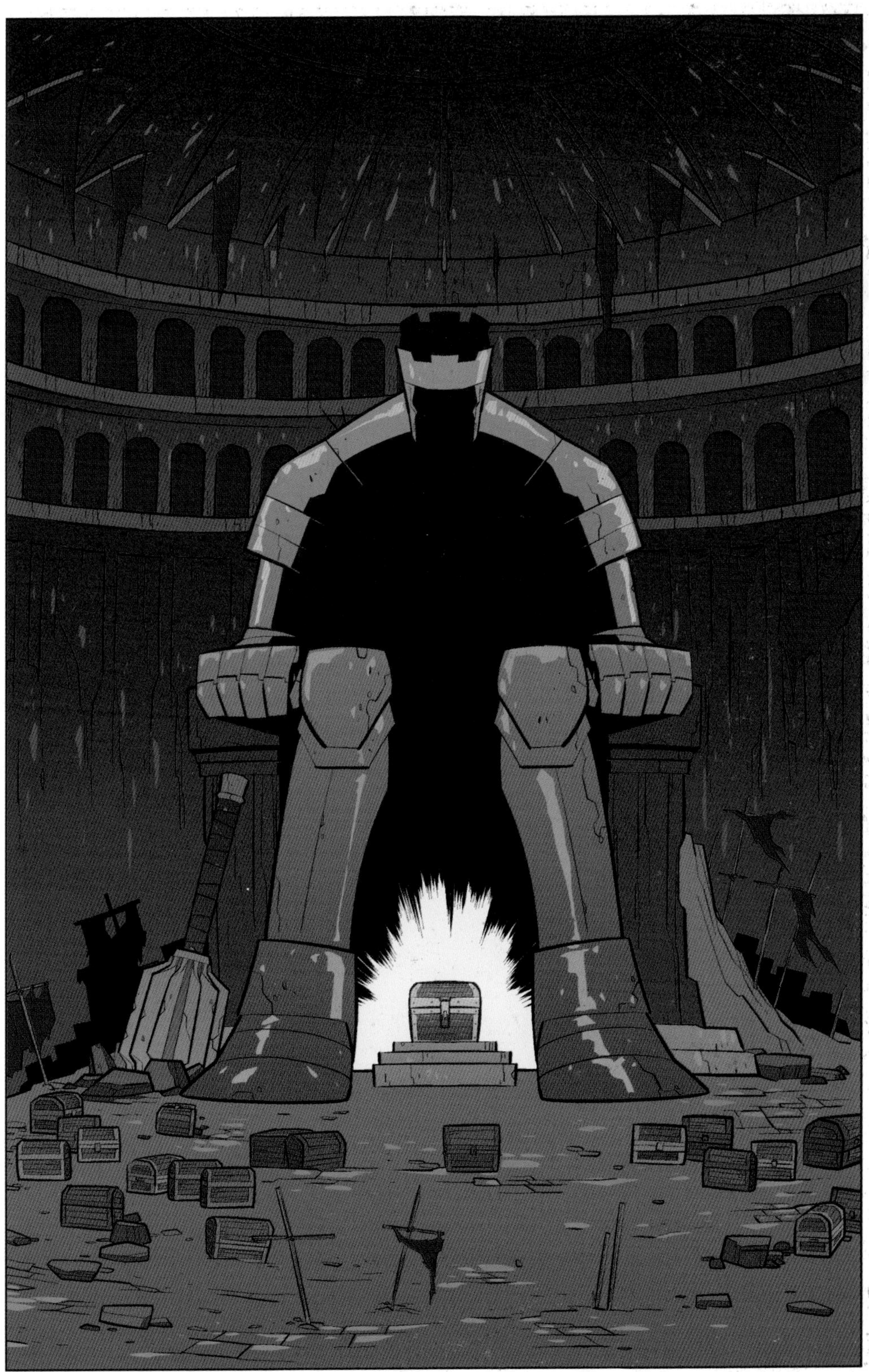

WE DON'T NEED TO FIGHT IT. ALL WE HAVE TO DO IS **SNEAK** BY IT.
I'VE GOT A WAY SIMPLER PLAN.

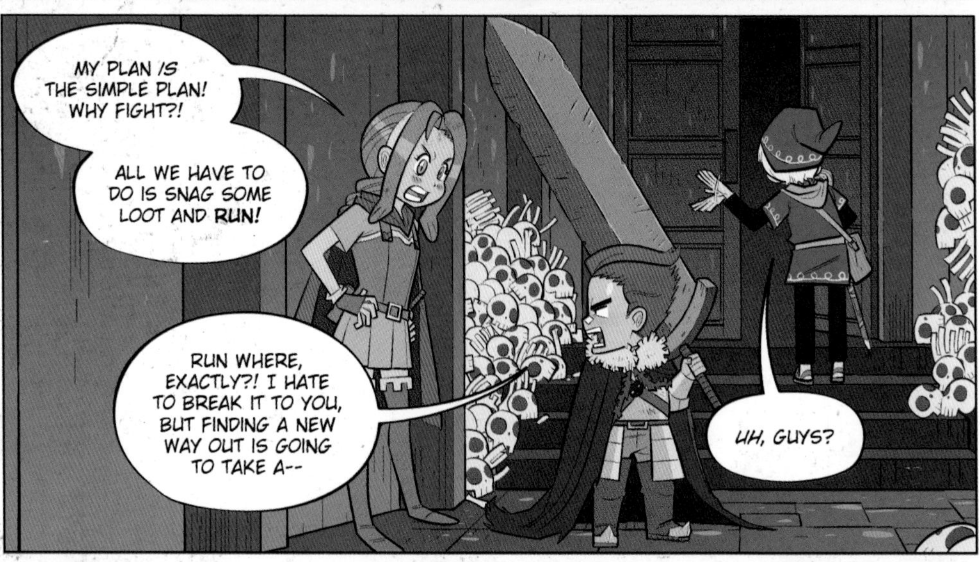
MY PLAN *IS* THE SIMPLE PLAN! WHY FIGHT?!
ALL WE HAVE TO DO IS SNAG SOME LOOT AND **RUN!**
RUN WHERE, EXACTLY?! I HATE TO BREAK IT TO YOU, BUT FINDING A NEW WAY OUT IS GOING TO TAKE A--
UH, GUYS?

GUYS.
WHAT?

IT'S ALREADY DEAD.

IN THAT CASE! LET'S START WITH THE BIGGEST, SHINIEST LOOT!
THIS ONE *DEFINITELY* LOOKS LIKE AN ARTIFACT CHEST TO ME.
IT LOOKS LOCKED. AND PROBABLY **BOOBY-TRAPPED.**

THANKFULLY, I HAPPEN TO BE AN **EXPERT** ON THIS SUBJECT.
JUST STAND BACK AND WATCH THE GREAT MANDY IN HER **NATURAL HABITAT!**

EE HEE HEE HEE!
DO YOU HEAR THAT?
QUIET. I NEED TO CONCENTRATE.

FWOOOOOOOOOO

OOOOOOOOOOOOO
UHHH...
I'VE GOT A
BAD FEELING
ABOUT THIS.

TWITCH

AAAGH!
QUIET!

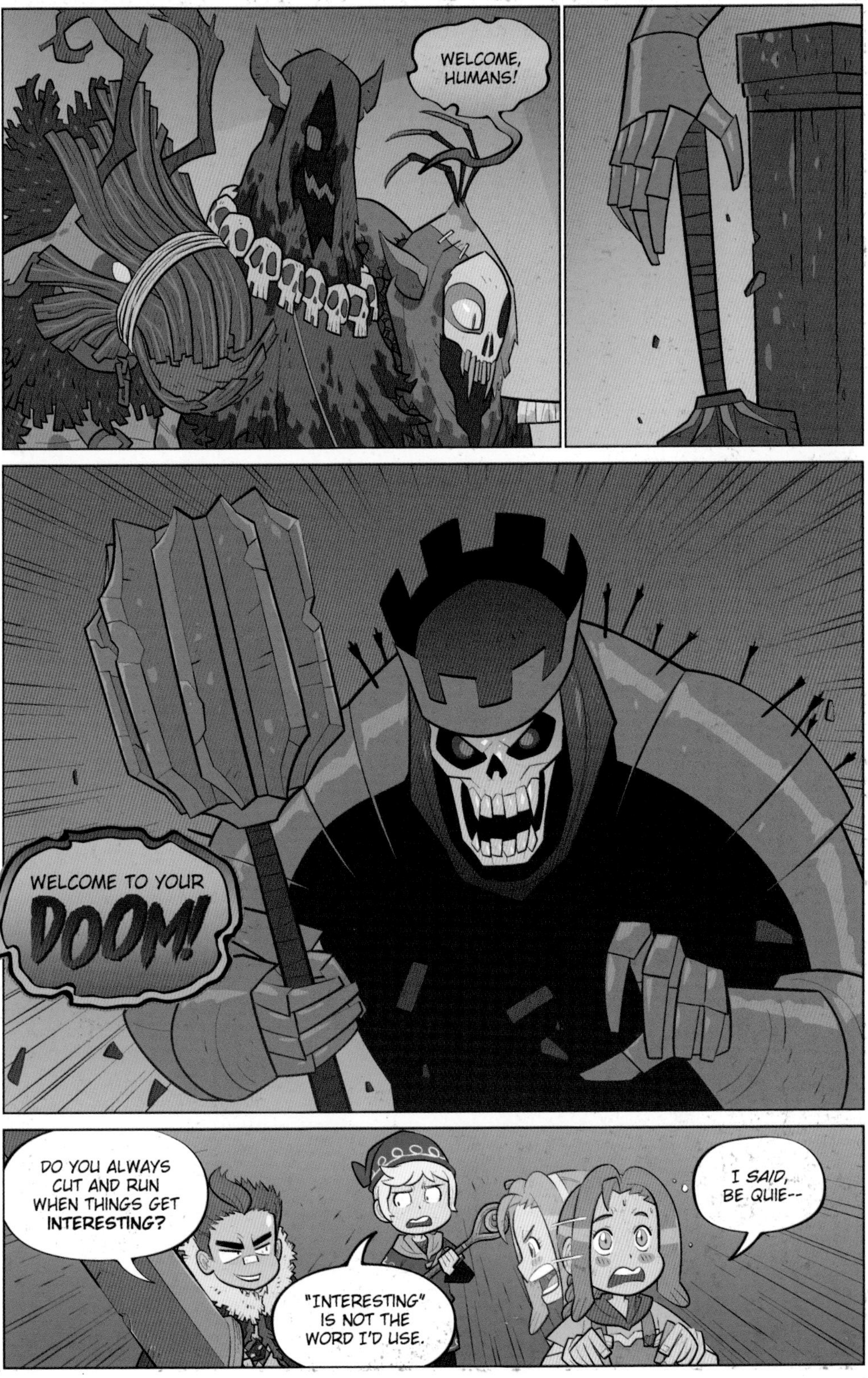

WELCOME TO YOUR DOOM!

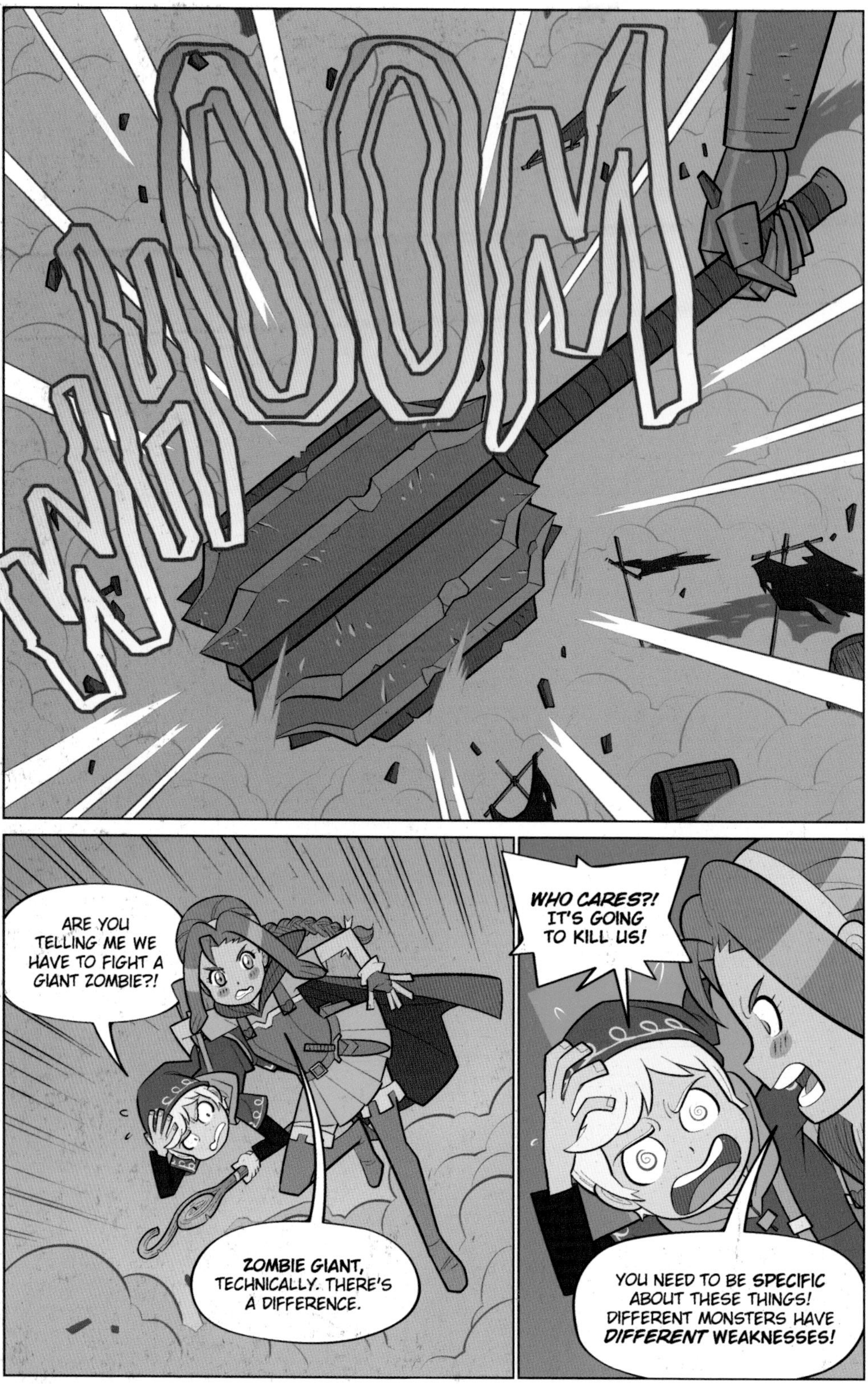

WHOOM

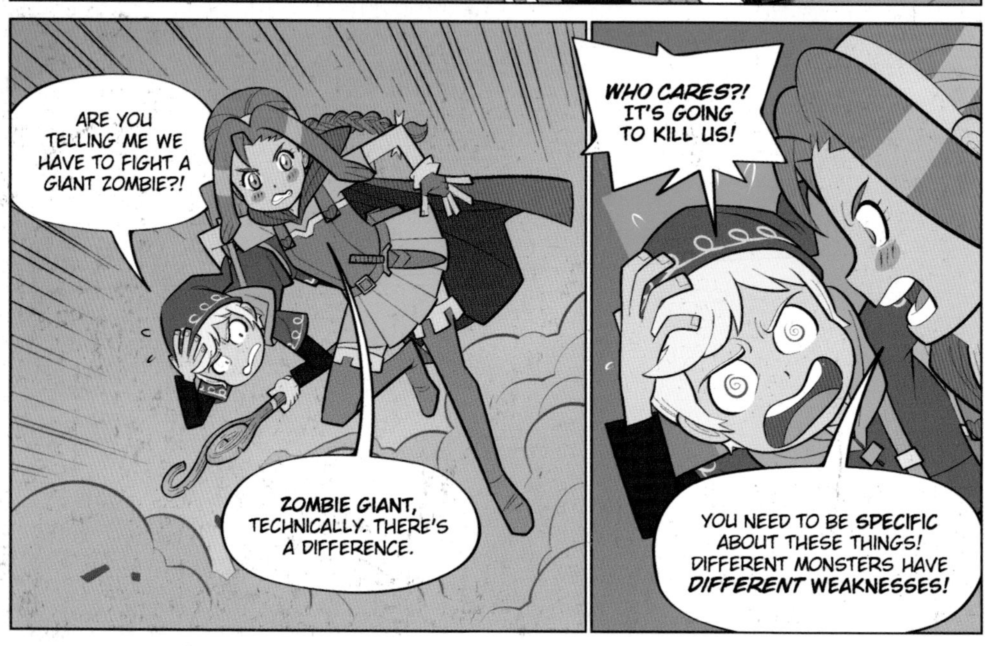

ARE YOU TELLING ME WE HAVE TO FIGHT A GIANT ZOMBIE?!
ZOMBIE GIANT, TECHNICALLY. THERE'S A DIFFERENCE.
WHO CARES?! IT'S GOING TO KILL US!
YOU NEED TO BE SPECIFIC ABOUT THESE THINGS! DIFFERENT MONSTERS HAVE DIFFERENT WEAKNESSES!

NO NEED TO FIGHT, SHE SAYS...!

CLANG
CLANG
CLANG

CLANG

JUST SNEAK BY, SHE SAYS...!

?!
SWOOSH

UH-OH...
TING

NEED A LITTLE HELP, ZACH?

EEP.

OOF!
TOSS
OOPSIE.

EEEEK!

PLUP
PLUP

AHHH.
IT'S GOOD TO
BE THE KING.

SLURRRP...

AS YOU
SAY, SIRE.

CRUNCH

SIRE! IF WE SQUISH
THE HUMANS, THEY
WON'T *COOK* WELL!

EH, WHO CARES
ABOUT THE MESS?
TRY TO ENJOY
THE SHOW!

TEAR
'EM APART,
BIG GUY!

WE NEED A PLAN!
OH, SURE! LET'S JUST ASK THE MONSTER FOR A QUICK ***TIME-OUT!***

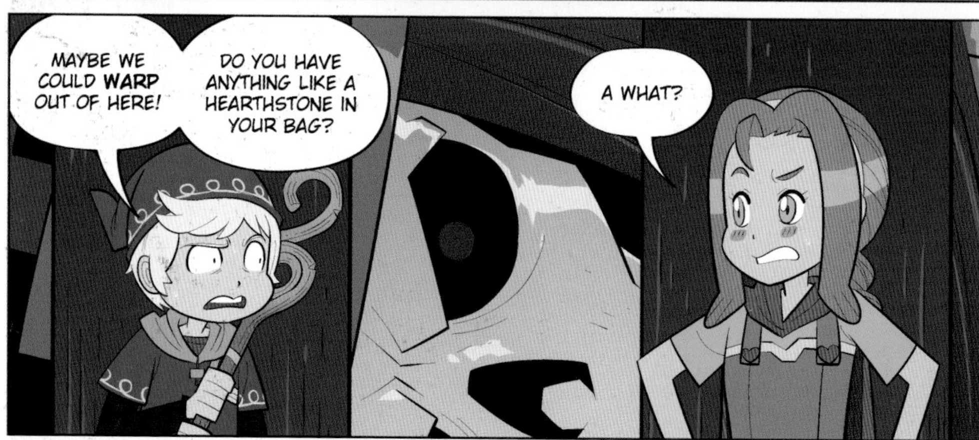
MAYBE WE COULD **WARP** OUT OF HERE!
DO YOU HAVE ANYTHING LIKE A HEARTHSTONE IN YOUR BAG?
A WHAT?

A SCROLL OF TOWN PORTAL!
HUH?
CLANK CLANK
CLANK
A WAND OF MARK AND RECALL?!
THIS ISN'T A ***VIDEO GAME,*** NATHAN! THIS IS REAL LIFE!

MAYBE IT'S GOT A **WEAK POINT** OR SOMETHING?!

FOCUS! HOW MANY **SPELLS** HAVE YOU GOT LEFT, NATHAN?!
J-J-JUST ONE! BUT I CAN'T THINK OF ANYTHING THAT WOULD--

HEY, UGLY! OVER HERE!
GROOOO...

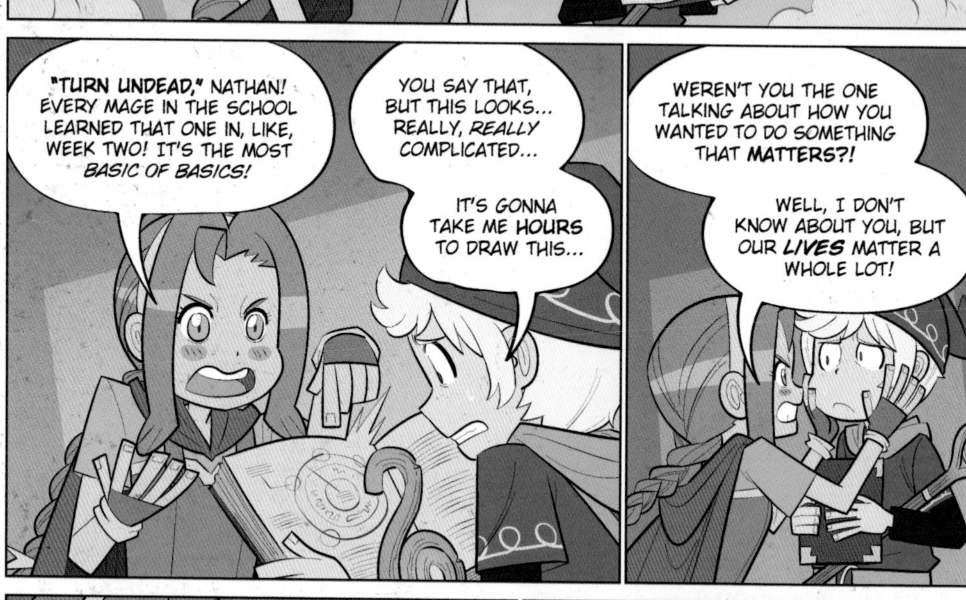

BE AWESOME. YOU GOT THIS!

WINK

CLENCH

I'LL NEED TIME.

CONCENTRATE... CONCENTRATE...

HAVE TO DO IT PERFECTLY...

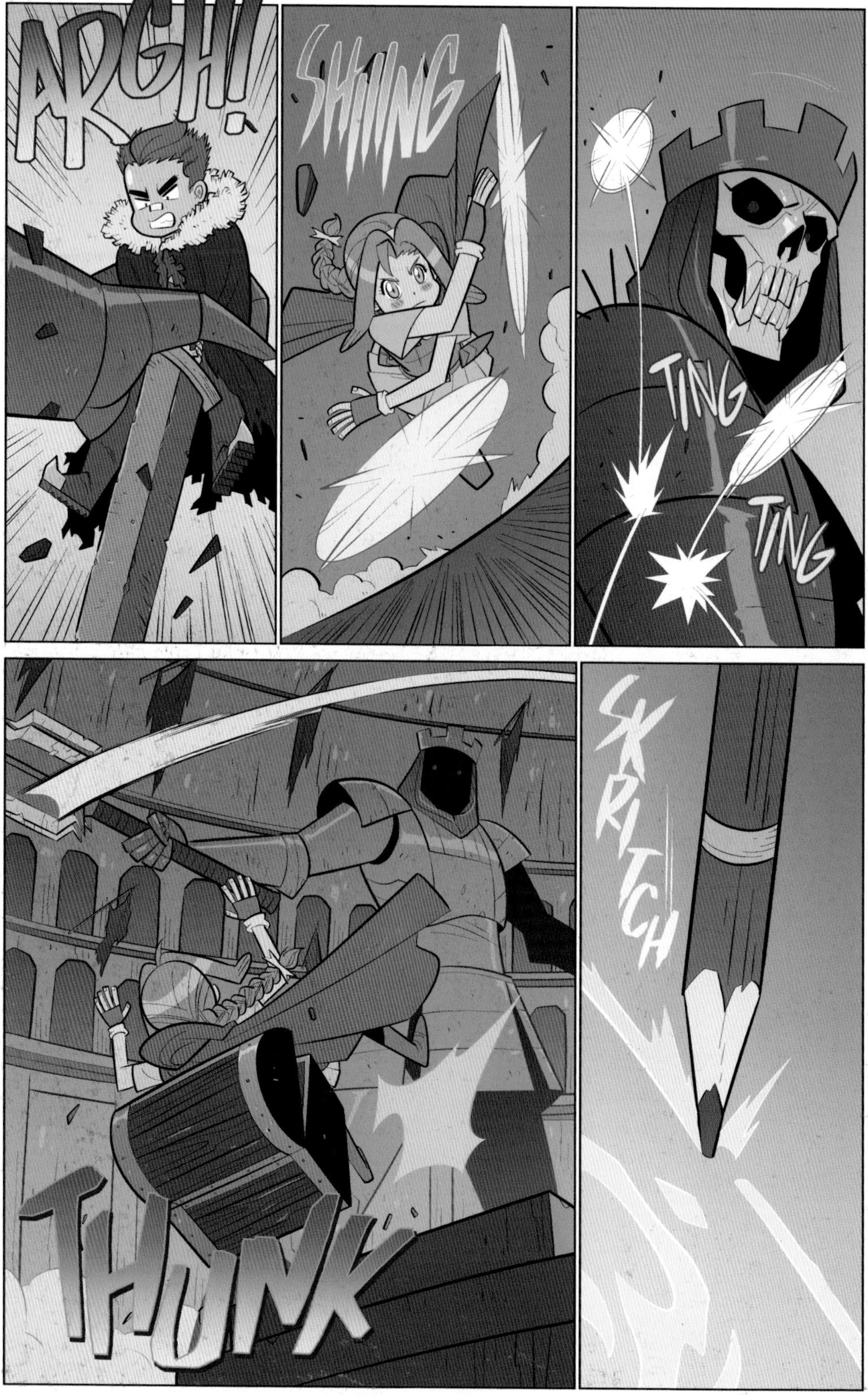

ARGH!

SHIIING

TING

TING

THUNK

SKRITCH

DOOM

COME ON...
COME ON...
WORK!

SHOOO
GREEE

GREEEEE!

WHAT WAS THAT LIGHT? IT ALMOST HAD THEM.
TELL THOSE NECROGOBLINS TO KEEP IT GOING!
AT ONCE, SIRE!

OH, DEAR.
GREEEEE!
THE LIGHT! CURSED, CURSED LIGHT!
IT BURNSES! IT BURNSES!

REEEEEEEEEE!
SIRE, PERHAPS WE SHOULD--

THOOM THOOM
UH-OH.
THOOM THOOM

DOOM

WHAM

OH, HEY, GUYS. NICE TIMING.
I WAS JUST GETTING READY TO COME **CHECK** ON YOU!
PHEW!
THUD

WAS THERE A PROBLEM?
"ONE OR TWO WEAK MONSTERS AT WORST," WAS THAT IT?

WE COULD'VE CARRIED A SMALLER BOX.
SEVERAL BOXES, EVEN.
THIS ONE WAS *CLEARLY* THE SHINIEST.
HEY, LOOKS LIKE YOU FOUND **TREASURE!** NICE JOB.

I DON'T KNOW ABOUT THESE TWO, BUT I ACTUALLY HAD A LOT OF FUN.
HEH!
WELL...
IT WAS AWFUL, BUT IF I GOT **LOOT**, THEN IT WAS A **FUN** KIND OF AWFUL.

THAT'S THE DUNGEON CRAWLER SPIRIT! LET'S GO HOME!
SO, WAS I AWESOME, OR WAS I AWESOME?
EH...PASSABLY AWESOME.

CHAPTER SIX

AFTER A VERY LONG WEEKEND...

THANKS FOR STAYING AFTER CLASS.
WE'VE FINISHED GOING OVER EVERYBODY'S REPORTS, AND TOMORROW, WE'LL OFFICIALLY UNVEIL ALL THE PERFORMANCE RANKINGS.

OOH, OOH! HOW DID WE DO?
IF YOU'RE TALKING TO US EARLY, I BET WE DID PRETTY GOOD.

WELL...

ALLOW ME TO REMIND YOU THAT I FOILED DEADLY TRAPS, RECOVERED PRICELESS TREASURE...
AND GAVE THIS GUY THE **COACHING** HE NEEDED TO PULL US ACROSS THE FINISH LINE!
AHA HAH! WELL, SHUCKS.

YOU'RE IN ***LAST PLACE.***

HUH?!

THIS WAS YOUR FIRST TRIP!
YOU FOUND CLEAR SIGNS OF MONSTER TERRITORY. AND INSTEAD OF TAKING THE TIME TO SCOUT THINGS OUT, YOU CHARGED *STRAIGHT INTO IT!*

UH, THAT'S KINDA TRUE, ACTUALLY.
NOW HOLD ON A--

YOU COULD HAVE AT LEAST CIRCLED BACK TO ASK **ENZO** FOR ADVICE!
WHY DO YOU THINK WE SENT HIM WITH YOU?
ABOUT THAT...

WE'RE TRAINING EXPLORERS AND HEROES!
NOT RECKLESS ADRENALINE JUNKIES WITH A DEATH WISH!
BUT WE WON!

BARELY! IF YOU KEEP COUNTING ON LUCK, YOU'RE NOT GOING TO SURVIVE IN THERE!
LAST PLACE! NO EXCUSES!
GRUMBLE GRUMBLE...

AND FOR THAT REASON, WE'LL HAVE A SPECIAL LECTURE ON SAFETY TOMORROW. DON'T BE LATE!
GROAN...

THIS SUCKS! I'M OUT OF HERE!
YOU SAID IT! I'M GOING TO TAKE THE WORLD'S LONGEST NAP!

OH, NATHAN! I ALMOST FORGOT. THEY'RE EXPECTING YOU AT THE APPRAISAL ROOM.

APPRAISAL?

THIS IS WHERE OUR EXPERTS **STUDY** THE ARTIFACTS BROUGHT OUT OF THE DUNGEON.

THEY FINISHED IT EARLIER TODAY. HEAD INTO THE BACK! OUR BEST APPRAISER IS WAITING FOR YOU.
UH, HELLO? YOU WANTED TO SEE ME?
LONG TIME NO SEE, KID. HOW'S MY FIVE MILLION DOLLAR **STAFF**?
MISTER VANCE!
UM...AM I IN TROUBLE?
HARDLY. TAKE A SEAT.

ACTUALLY, YOU REMIND ME OF CYRUS. BACK WHEN WE WERE KIDS.
WHICH IS A COMPLIMENT, BY THE WAY.
I ALREADY TOOK THE LIBERTY OF FIGURING OUT THE LOCK.
PLONK

WHOA! AWESOME!

I DON'T KNOW IF ANYBODY EXPLAINED HOW THIS WORKS TO YOU YET, BUT AS THE FINDERS OF AN ARTIFACT, YOU HAVE THE RIGHT TO DECIDE WHETHER IT GOES ON SALE, OR WHETHER YOU USE IT YOURSELVES.

REALLY? I SHOULD CHECK WITH MANDY AND ZACH.
THEY'RE NOT THE ONES WHO OWE ME FIVE MILLION DOLLARS.
ERR...! I'M ALL EARS, MISTER VANCE, SIR.

MY AUCTION COMPANY WOULD BE HAPPY TO SELL THIS FOR YOU, AND SINCE I LIKE YOU, WE'LL **WAIVE** THE USUAL BROKERAGE FEE.
UH, THAT'S GOOD, RIGHT?

BLAH
COUNTING THE OBLIGATORY FIVE PERCENT CONTRIBUTION TO SCHOOL OPERATING BUDGET, IGNORING THE BROKERAGE FEE, LESS FEDERAL TAXES (COMPLIANT WITH IRS TAX CODE SECTION 61 [TREASURY REGULATION §1.61-14(A)]), LESS STATE TAXES, AND SPLIT THREE WAYS WITH YOUR PARTNERS, IT AMOUNTS TO **TWO THOUSAND DOLLARS** GUARANTEED VALUATION WITH THE OUTSIDE CHANCE OF HIGHER REVENUE AT AUCTION.

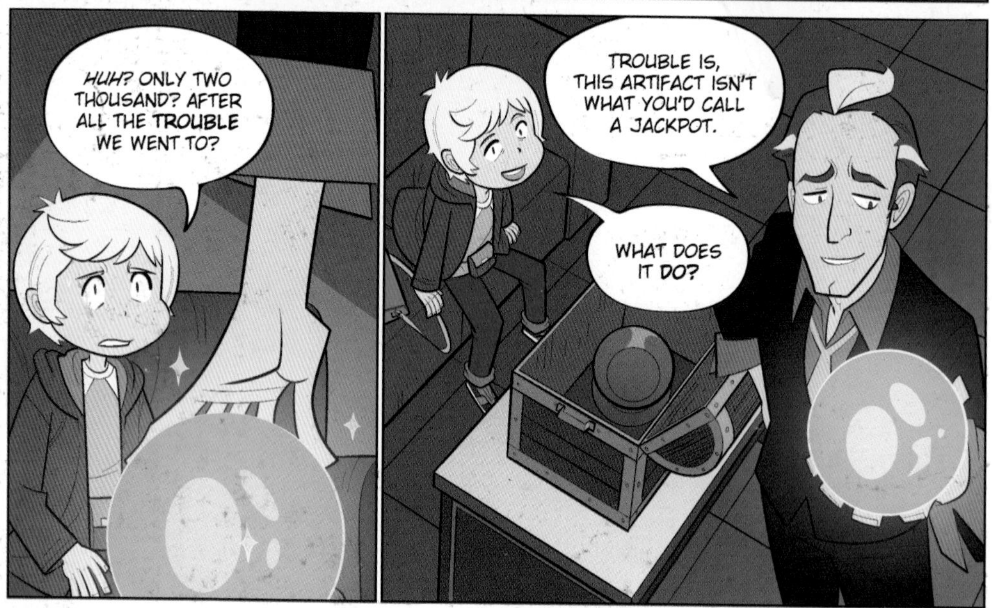
HUH? ONLY TWO THOUSAND? AFTER ALL THE **TROUBLE** WE WENT TO?
TROUBLE IS, THIS ARTIFACT ISN'T WHAT YOU'D CALL A JACKPOT.
WHAT DOES IT **DO?**

I'M THINKING OF CALLING IT "THE SNOW GLOBE OF STATELY SPRINKLES."
SHAKE SHAKE
AND WE FOUGHT A GIANT MONSTER OVER *THIS?* YEAH... JUST SELL IT.

TOUGH BREAK, HUH?
WIND

BUT THERE'S ALWAYS NEXT TIME! TAKE CARE, KID.
I HAVE A FEELING YOU'LL SHOW ME GRANDER TREASURES AFTER YOUR *NEXT* ADVENTURE.
SNAP
POOMF

UUUUGH!
AND SO BEGAN MY LIFE AS AN ADVENTURER.

Meanwhile, in the heart of goblin town...

NO. IT'S BECAUSE I DON'T WANT THERE TO BE ANY **PROBLEMS!**
W-WE SENT THEM PACKING, MASTER COWL, SIR! THOSE HUMANS WON'T SHOW THEIR FACES AROUND HERE EVER AGAIN!
YOU'D BETTER *HOPE* THAT'S TRUE. BECAUSE IF THE **DUNGEON MASTER** FINDS OUT WE FAILED TO PROTECT OUR TREASURES...!
TH-THE DUNGEON MASTER WOULD NEVER COME HERE. H-HE'S GOT MUCH MORE IMPORTANT THINGS TO DO.

SKRE

OH, NO.

CLOM

THAP

MY LORD.
I CAN EXPLAIN! I CAN EXPLAIN EVERYTHING!

I-I-IT'S REALLY HIM...!
QUIET.
Y-YES, MY LORD.
LISTEN CAREFULLY, BECAUSE I'M NOT GOING TO REPEAT MYSELF.

YOU'RE GOING TO **FIND** SOMEONE FOR ME.
FIND THIS GIRL. SEIZE HER. AND BRING HER TO ME. **ALIVE**.
RUSTLE

THE HUMANS
WILL BE BACK.
THEY *ALWAYS*
COME BACK.
I'VE BEEN
HANDS-OFF FOR
FAR TOO LONG.

IT'S TIME TO BRING THIS DUNGEON BACK TO LIFE.
TO BE CONTINUED

The Adventure continues in

DUNGEON CRAWLERS ACADEMY

BOOK TWO

THE DRAGON'S TREASURE

COMING SOON!

DUNGEON CRAWLERS ACADEMY

OUR CURRICULUM

So you want to be a hero? Come to the original school for adventurers! Dungeon Crawlers Academy is built right on top of the portal to the Dungeon in picturesque upstate New York. Nearby is the quirkiest town in the U.S.—there's more magic here than anywhere else in the world!

We're always accepting applicants for the freshman class: visit a recruiting station in any major city!

With a full course load spanning grades 9-12, our Academy offers a fully accredited college preparatory education. (And also teaches you how to slay monsters! What more could you want?)

COURSES

Dungeoneering

In this class, students learn all the survival skills they need to deal with a hostile otherworldly environment. Whether it's navigating traps, learning which mushrooms are poisonous, or how to get by when there's no light source, our instructors have it covered.

Teacher: GARRET McGOWAN

Combat & Athletics:

While not every student is a natural fighter, all of them need a little practice in how to deal with the deadly creatures that roam the dungeon. This program can feel a little strenuous compared to a normal P.E. program. Be prepared to sweat!

Teacher: DIRK SWANK

Monsterology:

With our menagerie of real live monster specimens captured for study, our Academy is a world leader in figuring out what makes monsters tick. A student well-versed in monsterology is better poised to defeat the creatures in the Dungeon.

Teacher: ANNABELLE WILLIS

Math, Science, & the Humanities:

Standard academic subjects are also taught at our Academy. The added course load may be a challenge, but no one said being an adventurer was easy. The Academy's AP science classes are nationally competitive.

SPECIALIZED CLASSES

Magic:

Any student with the talent for magic is obliged to attend Mage Class and master the runes they need to create active spells. The amount of memorization required is enormous, and magic is a deeply complicated art.

Teacher: MAXIMILIAN DONENSTONE

Skullduggery & Legerdemain:

Locked doors, hidden compartments, sealed chests, and dangerous pitfalls abound in the dungeon. Don't be fooled by the fancy name: this class is all about training up treasure thieves and tomb raiders.

Teacher: OLGA WAGNER

Advanced Combat:

Those with a knack for swinging swords train like Spartans in this uncompromising course, which seeks to turn the most promising fighters into masters of the blade. Every kind of blade, in fact. True fighters are comfortable with any weapon.

Teacher: School Headmaster, CYRUS WALKER

TOO YOUNG FOR THE REAL DEAL? CONSIDER DUNGEON PREP!

While only children can enter the Portal, let's face it: the Dungeon is no place to be crying for mommy or daddy. Our Academy conducts early training at our adjacent lower school campus for grades 5 through 8. Graduating from this program puts you on the fast track to the Academy. Only a few dozen students with exceptional talent are accepted each year.

If you think you have what it takes, apply today!

About the Writer

As an editor at manga publisher Seven Seas Entertainment, **J.P. Sullivan** has helped bring hundreds of volumes of Japanese media to English-speaking audiences. His original science fiction and fantasy has been published in magazines like *Podcastle* and *Beneath Ceaseless Skies*; he is also a graduate of the Clarion Writers' Workshop and grand prize winner of Baen's Fantasy Adventure Contest. Holder of a master's degree in international affairs from the American University, he currently lives in Los Angeles, but hopes to escape this reality through the nearest interdimensional portal.

About the Artist

Elmer Damaso has been a comic book illustrator since 2000, and has worked on such titles as Seven Seas Entertainment's *Speed Racer*, Lego/DC's *Hero Factory*, Dynamite Comics' *Robotech/Voltron*, and Titan Comics' *Robotech Remix*.